T0266945

THE
LIONS'
DEN

IRIS MWANZA

THE LIONS' DEN

GRAYDON
HOUSE

GRAYDON
HOUSE®

ISBN-13: 978-1-525-81954-4

The Lions' Den

Graydon House
22 Adelaide St. West, 41st Floor
Toronto, Ontario M5H 4E3, Canada
www.GraydonHouseBooks.com

Printed in U.S.A.

For David

The king declared to Daniel, "O Daniel, servant of the living God, has your God, whom you serve continually, been able to deliver from the lions?" Then Daniel said to the king, "O king, live forever! My God sent his angel and shut the lions' mouths, and they have not harmed me, because I was found blameless before him; and also before you, O king, I have done no harm."

Daniel 6:20–22

Lusaka

October 1990

1

Grace paused outside the maw of the Central Police Station. She'd passed this station five days a week going to and from work, but had never been inside. From the bus, Grace had admired its colonial architecture: the arched entrance, the imposing columns and the white, sweeping stairway that gleamed in the early morning sun. Now, surveying the building from up close, she could see that this once-grand building had gone to seed. Termites had cracked the facade and left dirty brown trails across the walls, weeds poked out of cracks and crevices in the stairs, and a determined ivy had crept halfway up one of the columns.

The decrepit building did nothing to dampen Grace's excitement. She had spent four years studying law, and the last five months at the firm of DB & Associates proofing legal documents. Now, finally, she had been given a case. It was a pro bono criminal case that no one else wanted but still… Grace suppressed a smile and stepped from the sunlight into the building's gloomy entrance.

A policeman sat in the foyer behind a mukwa wood desk, almost hidden behind manila folders in messy piles.

"I'm here to see my client, Willbess Mulenga," Grace said to the officer. He lifted up his head, took off his glasses and pointed his lenses at Grace as if she were a bug to be magnified. Knowing that her habit of looking people in the eye was considered bad manners, she looked down into her bag and pretended to dig for something, careful not to squash her banana. When she looked up again, the policeman was still staring at her. His glasses were perched back on his broad nose, and his magnified eyes gave him a comical look, but his lips were thin and unsmiling. He pulled out a manila folder from one of the piles and opened it over the newspaper on his desk, covering the full-page color pictorial of President Kaunda in his Chairman Mao suit waving a white handkerchief to crowds. It looked like yesterday's paper, but the newspapers were always full of fetching pictures of the President so Grace couldn't be sure. She cleared her throat a few times, but the policeman continued to ignore her.

"I'm a lawyer from DB & Associates," she said, surprised at how tinny her voice sounded. The policeman stretched and yawned, exposing the dark patches under his arms, before extracting a form from his desk drawer and handing it to Grace. The form had been photocopied to the faintness of a spider web, and it took Grace several minutes to figure out the questions and fill it in. She gave it back to the policeman, who reviewed her answers, his lips moving as he read.

"Grace Zulu," the officer whispered, reading her name off the bottom of the form. "Zulu," he repeated loudly. "My sister, you're from Eastern Province?" He was suddenly all smiles. "Which village?"

How did he know that I'm from the village? Grace wondered in dismay. Maybe it was her second-hand skirt suit. Or maybe it was the cicatrices on her cheeks. Grace ran her fingers over the ndembo left by the nganga's razorblade and the black potion he had rubbed into the fresh cuts—protection from evil spirits, her father had told her.

"Chief Nyamphande's village."

The man switched from English to Nsenga. "I'm Officer Lungu from Chief Mumbi's village, less than forty kilometers from Nyamphande. You must know it."

"Ndithu," she nodded. Clans from the two villages had intermarried for generations. She had even been there with her father, but it was so long ago she couldn't remember why. She recalled walking through fields of maize, millet and sorghum, across a stick bridge over the Nyakawise river, up and along a series of waterfalls in the Chibulubulu hills, and then finally down a winding dirt path, only to arrive at a village that looked exactly like Nyamphande— mud huts with neatly thatched roofs, surrounded by fields of maize, millet and sorghum.

Grace switched back to English. She was here for work, not fraternizing. "Officer, I'm in a hurry to see my client."

"Iai. You must wait for approval."

"Approval? I have a legal right to see my client."

"Ndithu, but there are still procedures to follow."

Grace thought about her boss, Avaristo. She couldn't go back to the office without getting this interview done. Avaristo always expressed his opinions at high volume. She imagined his reaction if she offered Officer Lungu as an excuse. *What moron can't execute a basic client interview? Get out and don't come back until you've done your job!*

"I need to see my client today," Grace insisted.

The policeman shook his head and said, "As you can see, there are many in line before you," pointing to the piles on his desk. "But since you are in a big hurry, sisi, pay the expediting fee and I'll see what I can do."

All Grace had in her bag was ten kwacha—her bus fare for the rest of the week—and a banana. Even if she did have the money, she wasn't about to pay a bribe. "I've never heard of any such fee."

Officer Lungu shrugged. "DB & Associates has lots of money, sisi, tell your bosses not to be so stingy."

Grace wished he would stop calling her his sister. She opened her mouth, but then shut it again before saying a word. She knew reason wouldn't work on a corrupt cop; she would wait for his shift to end and start again with the next policeman, and would file a complaint against Officer Lungu—one rotten egg made the whole police force look bad. As she turned to walk away, Officer Lungu stood up and called her back: "Sisi! Bwela, bwela, bwela!" Standing, Officer Lungu was surprisingly short, his uniform ill-fitting and a size too small, but he wasn't as corpulent as his big head had suggested. "I'll help you today, but next time you must bring me a token of appreciation. You understand?" He didn't wait for an answer. "Follow me."

Grace hesitated; she didn't want to owe Officer Lungu anything, but then thought about Avaristo and raced after him, her kitten heels clicking against the concrete floor. She followed him down a long corridor to the left, past several women sitting on a bench who looked up hopefully, but the policeman ignored them. Grace felt guilty walking in Officer Lungu's wake past these dejected-looking women in their bright blouses and chitenge, the colorful cloths tied at the waist and covering them down to their ankles. She didn't need to be told that they were waiting to see their husbands and sons, and wondered if the police required "appreciation" from them before letting them in.

Around the next corner, Officer Lungu paused and held up his fist for her to stop, peered up a narrow stairway, then skipped across it. "Hurry now," he whispered, moving even faster around yet another corner and into an unlit corridor. A fluorescent light above them suddenly buzzed on and startled Grace, but Officer Lungu didn't seem to notice. "You're tall like a giraffe, and just as beautiful," he said to Grace over his shoulder. She ignored him. She knew she was too tall, too dark and too thin to be beautiful. At over six feet, she particularly hated being compared to a giraffe.

"Are you married?"

"I'm not interested."

"In marriage or in me?" Officer Lungu stopped at a door at the end of this last long corridor.

"Neither."

He laughed. "Ah, but you girls of nowadays, mukonda kumeka."

How dare he think I'm playing hard to get! Grace thought, but said nothing, fearing that any word she uttered would reveal how much she already despised this little, toad-like policeman. Officer Lungu opened the door and said, "Wait in here."

2

To Grace's relief, it was an interview room with no prison cells in sight. She had heard that the cells were so over-crowded that prisoners had to arrange themselves head to toe, like sardines, to sleep. This room was small with high ceilings and three tiny windows at the top of one wall shafting light into the gloom. In the middle of the room were two wooden chairs on either side of a narrow metal table, with a drawer hanging out like a dog's tongue. Grace pushed in the drawer, but it rolled out again. After a few shoves, she gave up and sat down. She pulled out the case sheet, a legal pad and two pens, and arranged and rear-ranged the items on the desk while she waited for her client.

Although she knew it by heart, she reviewed the case sheet now tucked inside her legal pad:

Name: Willbess Mulenga of Plot 847/11/9, Kalikiliki Township

Charges: Contravening Section 155 of the Penal Code

Age: Unknown

Details: After an incident reported on the night of September 15, 1990, at the MacGyver Bar, one Willbess
Mulenga, a male dressed as a female, was reported to
have been seen in flagrante delicto with an unknown
male patron. Willbess Mulenga was arrested the morning of September 16, 1990, at his parents' home in
Kalikiliki.

Grace had loved criminal law in school, puzzling over labyrinthine codes, Latin phrases and shifting burdens of proof.
She had even interviewed with the Public Defender's Office,
but withdrew when they told her they required a year as an
unpaid intern, which she couldn't afford. She didn't earn very
much as a first-year at DB & Associates, but it was enough,
exactly enough to pay her room and board, transport costs
and to send 100 kwacha back to her mother in the village
every month. Although the firm was corporate, it did have a
small portfolio of pro bono criminal cases. Grace had found
a copy of the green-velour-covered Penal Code in the firm's
library and had flipped through it until she found Section 155:
"Any person who has carnal knowledge of any person against
the order of nature; or permits a male person to have carnal

knowledge…against the order of nature; is guilty of a felony
and is liable to imprisonment for fourteen years."

As Grace waited for her client, she pondered the meaning
of "the order of nature." Homosexuality was part of nature,
of that she was sure. She had seen it in both the animal and
human worlds, and so read Section 155 as an effort to rewrite the laws of nature. Grace thought about Mr. Patel.
He had been her father's oldest and dearest friend. No one
told her that Mr. Patel was different, it was just something
she came to understand as she got older, but, unlike most
of the village, it didn't change how much she loved him.
She didn't understand why anyone cared about his private
life, but they did. He was rejected by his family, and, with
the exception of her father, demonized and mistreated by
the villagers. And now, an even worse fate awaited her client, imprisoned and in remand since mid-September. More
than four weeks already!

Grace made a note in the margin: "Research constitutional challenges to Penal Code, Sec. 155—rights to
privacy/protections from discrimination." She slid her finger a few inches down the page. She circled Willbess's
age, noted as "Unknown." Were these consenting adults?
The age of consent was sixteen. And what about the other
facts? Not much on record except a male dressed as a female caught *in flagrante delicto* with another male in a bar.
"In flagrante delicto, a blazing offence," she whispered.
Who were the witnesses to this blazing offence? Why was
Willbess wearing a dress? The burden of proof was on the
prosecution but she still needed the facts. She thought about

her old professor Dzekedzeke's favorite legal aphorism, "If you have the law, hammer the law. If you have the facts, hammer the facts. And if you have neither the law nor the facts, hammer the table." Grace pretended to hammer the metal table.

The squares of light streaming into the room through the small box-windows crept across the floor. What was taking so long? Grace was hungry, and started to think about the fruit in her bag. Her growling stomach was audible but she couldn't risk her client walking in as she stuffed a banana into her mouth. The room was tinged red by the setting sun and she was about to give up and leave when Officer Lungu burst in with what appeared to be a boy, and gave him a quick shove into the empty seat.

"Your client," Officer Lungu said, looking as pleased as if he had performed a magic trick. Grace stared at Willbess Mulenga in shock. He was even shorter than Officer Lungu, with a twig-like neck, and the thinnest arms and ankles sticking out of a stained red t-shirt and oversized prison-issue black pants. His light skin was bruised on the right side of his face, his right eye swollen shut and one of the two front teeth that seemed too big for his mouth was badly chipped. The smell of piss and shit was so strong that Grace gagged. Her manners forgotten, she yanked her handkerchief from her bag to cover her nose.

"Hands where I can see them," Officer Lungu growled. Willbess placed both small hands on the table. He had

black rings from handcuffs around his delicate wrists and
his hands were trembling.

"What happened to him?" Grace shouted at Officer
Lungu through her handkerchief.

"He resisted arrest. Looks worse than it is. Tell the nice
lady that you're fine."

The boy kept his head down and said nothing.

"He was arrested almost five weeks ago. These injuries
are fresh."

"So you're a doctor now?" The officer placed his boot
against the wall and pulled his truncheon from its loop in
his belt, spun it and then returned it. Willbess flinched.

Grace tried to control her rising anger. "My name is
Grace Zulu," she said to Willbess. "I'm your lawyer, and
I'm here to help you." She turned to Officer Lungu. "I wish
to speak to my client alone." She expected the policeman
to leave the room, but instead he moved closer to Willbess,
his squat body blocking the fading light. The boy started to
shiver despite the heat, and tears spilled out of his good eye.

Grace handed him her handkerchief, and as he took it,
their eyes met for a split-second. She jolted in her seat as if
an electric shock had run through her body, and for a moment she felt the full force of this boy's anguish and terror.
Grace had a strong urge to hold Willbess, to comfort and
reassure him that she would save him from this wretched
place, and that everything would be all right. She even
reached out to touch him but his hands were already in
his lap. Grace searched his broken face again to be certain
that she didn't know him, as she tried to understand this

sudden, strong instinct to protect him that felt more primal than lawyerly. Perhaps she identified with the suffering so clear in his one good eye, or perhaps it was recognition that their lives were equally precarious and only the thinnest, invisible line put Grace on this side of the table of misfortune and Willbess on the other. Grace shook off these strange sensations, reminding herself that she was there as his lawyer. She drew a sharp breath before she spoke, while glaring at Officer Lungu. "You have the right to speak to your lawyer in private, and you have the right to be treated with human dignity. The police have no right to beat you up." She glanced back at Willbess as she said, "They *will* answer for this."

Officer Lungu's big eyes narrowed behind his glasses. "Answer for what? I told you, he resisted arrest. I do you a favor and let you in, and now you want to start trouble?"

"I have every right to interview my client, it's not a favor."

"This interview is over." The policeman turned to Willbess. "Iwe! Get up!"

"You end this interview and I'm going to file an official complaint against you for police brutality, and for soliciting a bribe."

Officer Lungu sucked his teeth at Grace and then turned to Willbess and roared in his ear, "I said get up!" When Willbess didn't move, the policeman grabbed him by the neck and lifted him off the chair. Without thinking, Grace pounced to pull the officer off the boy.

"*Voetsek!*" screamed the policeman as he twisted and

shoved Grace with such force that she stumbled back, flipped over her chair and hit her head on the concrete floor.

When Grace came to, she immediately looked for Willbess but found that the small darkening room was empty. She untangled herself from the chair, put it right side up and then used it to pull herself off the floor and onto the seat. She touched the back of her head carefully and then felt around the base of her skull, where pain radiated. She checked her fingers for blood, but there was none. She stood up and pressed various points around her ribs; her left side was tender, but it didn't feel like anything was cracked or broken.

Grace tried to figure out how long she had been knocked out; the sky was still glowing red through the three windows so it couldn't have been long. She jumped when the fluorescent light in the corridor buzzed on. I need to get out of here! she thought and grabbed her papers off the floor and stuffed them into her bag as quickly as she could. With the bag slung on her shoulder, she pushed the door fully open with her foot and stepped out cautiously with her fists raised and her elbows tucked in as her father had taught her. The corridor was empty; there was no sign of Officer Lungu and no sign of her client.

3

Grace walked into her boss's office without knocking. Before she could speak, Avaristo held his right hand up to stop her. He continued to slash at a legal brief with his red pen in one hand while rubbing the wrinkles on his forehead with the other. Avaristo was decisively ugly, his nose too hooked, his chin too weak and his eyes far apart like a fish. Perhaps because he was so unattractive, his clothes were always impeccable. Even now, at the end of a hot October day, he looked pristine in a grey pinstriped suit, a crisp pink shirt and a purple silk tie in a tight Windsor knot at his throat. Grace felt shabby next to him at the best of times. She took a few ineffectual swipes at her filthy suit, then pressed down her hair. It had been carefully coiffed in the morning but now stood straight up like spikes on a porcupine. Avaristo continued to scribble and mutter "moron" several times in his strong English accent.

"Mr. Daka!" Grace didn't quite shout but she called out loud enough for him to snap his head up.

"Bloody hell! What happened to you?"

Grace shook her head in response. She tried to blink back her tears, but they spilled out and rolled down her face. She wanted to explain that she wasn't crying, she wasn't the crying type, she was angry. The last time was many years ago at her father's funeral, but thinking about that event made her tears run even faster. She covered her face with her hands.

"Oh for Christ's sake." Avaristo's words were as harsh as ever but his tone was gentle. She heard the chair legs scrape against the parquet floor, then felt Avaristo's hands on her shoulders, guiding her to the chair on the other side of his glass desk. "Sit. I'll get some tea." Grace could hear him opening doors down the hall, looking for reinforcements, but everyone else had already left the office. She fished around her bag for her handkerchief, but then remembered that she had given it to Willbess. Shamu! It was her favorite thing, heavy silk with a leopard jumping across a blue night sky full of planets and stars on one side, and a leopard print of pink spots on the other. She would never have bought herself such a luxurious item; she had found it in the inner pocket of her suit, purchased after much haggling at the second-hand clothes market. She liked the motif; leopards were an omen of death but not a bad omen—they were escorts taking the spirits of the dead safely to their ancestors. Grace didn't think of herself as superstitious; she had always known the spirit world and felt it when the ancestors were close.

She wanted her handkerchief back. It was the only beautiful and extravagant thing that she owned. She felt guilty for worrying about it being ruined by bloodstains, and then felt worse thinking that Officer Lungu might have taken it. Grace wiped her tears away with her palms like a child. Shamu! She inhaled back mucus and pinched her nose. The smell of overripe banana coming from her open bag made her realize that she was ravenous. It would probably be battered and bruised too, but she didn't care, she would eat it as soon as she got out of Avaristo's office. When her boss returned, he sniffed the air before handing her a mug of milky tea.

"Sorry, I found powdered milk but couldn't find any sugar. It's like gold now with these damned shortages. I did find a couple of biscuits." He handed her a long rectangular box with two biscuits in the bottom. Grace crammed them both into her mouth and slurped at her tea, enjoying the sweet, mealy pulp. She felt better almost immediately.

"If this is a domestic issue, you know the firm can't get—"

"It was the police," Grace interrupted with her mouth still full. She swallowed and then continued, "A policeman roughed up my client right in front of me, and then shoved me to the ground! I'm going to file an official complaint against Officer Lungu tomorrow."

"What? Wait, which client?"

"Willbess Mulenga."

Avaristo looked back at her blankly.

"The boy accused of committing acts against the order of nature."

Avaristo pursed his lips and widened his fish eyes. Grace cleared her throat before stating, "The Penal Code for homosexual sex." She had never said "homosexual sex" out loud before, much less to her boss. Her cheeks burned.

"Ah right, that poof case," Avaristo said without any apparent malice. She hadn't heard that word before, but coming from him, she guessed it was pejorative. Grace had once dared to complain about his language and he had responded with a wide grin. "You're a ballsy one, aren't you? If I were you, I'd worry less about my language and more about what I'm trying to drum into your thick skull."

Avaristo reached over for a notepad and pen, and half sat on the desk next to her. "Tell me exactly what happened."

Grace explained while he scratched at his notepad. She tried to suppress her anger and sound matter-of-fact, dispassionate, lawyerly. When Grace told him how Officer Lungu had shoved her to the ground and knocked her out, Avaristo stopped writing. "Jesus H. Christ! A doctor should take a look at you." He walked around her to examine her head and it took several minutes of Grace insisting that she was fine before he sat down and let her resume the story.

When she was done talking, Avaristo seemed to keep rereading what he had written down before he finally spoke. "So, you didn't have the right paperwork but Officer Lungu nevertheless allowed you to interview your client and then—" he paused and sighed "—without any corroborating evidence, you accused the policeman of beating up your client and then assaulted said policeman as he attempted to remove his prisoner from the interrogation room."

"That's not what I said at all!" Grace wailed.

"That's how the commissioner will interpret this." He dropped his notepad on the desk. "In case you didn't know it, he's an ex-cop who *will* take Officer Lungu's side."

"So you're not going to help me with Officer Lungu?"

"I am trying to help you. Listen to me, let's get the client out of police custody before making angry noises to the Police Complaints Commissioner."

"They won't dare touch him now that he has us as his lawyers."

"Right. I'm sure it slipped Officer Lungu's mind just this one time."

Grace wrapped her head in her arms and slumped onto the desk. She wished this miserable day would end, and she really wished that Avaristo would stop being a sarcastic jerk for one minute. As if he heard what she was thinking, Avaristo's voice softened. "It's been a difficult day for me too. I'm really under the cosh with DB out sick. I'm not sure when he'll be back—that's if he'll be back."

Grace reared up. "What do you mean?" DB was the firm. His name was on the door. He had made his name defending President Kaunda during the independence struggle and had built the firm over the last twenty-six years into the best in the country. He was as patient and as gentlemanly as Avaristo was short-tempered and rude. Grace was assigned to DB, but he had gone on sick leave almost as soon as she had started the job. Working for Avaristo was supposed to be temporary.

"Nothing. Nothing for you to worry about. DB will be back soon enough," Avaristo said while he reached into his back pocket, retrieved his wallet and pulled out some kwacha. "Here's some cash for a taxi. Go home, Grace, and get some rest over the weekend. Come Monday, I'll have another associate take over the case."

Grace banged the desk. "No! This is my case!" she shouted.

"Listen here, young lady! It's the firm's case and it was my mistake to give it to you before you were ready." Avaristo's voice was becoming high-pitched and Grace could see that the sympathy in his eyes had evaporated.

"I'm sorry, sir. I've handled things badly but please don't take me off this case," she begged. Grace knew that none of the other associates would fight hard for Willbess; in fact they had all fought *not* to take this case. "*Non me!*" the five other associates had all shouted, laughing. Mabvuto, her office mate, explained that it was Latin for "Not me, " and that pro bono cases went to the last man, or, now that she was on board, the last person to say it. "But I want this case!" she had responded, and was delighted when Avaristo declared the matter settled.

"My client—I mean *our* client is in a bad way. He's just a boy and he's been beaten and I feel..." How could she explain it to Avaristo? He derided anything unempirical and would dismiss her entirely if she said that she had actually felt his terror, and that she knew she would have no respite until he was safe. Instead Grace simply said, "I feel responsible for him."

"Well, you're not personally responsible for anyone. Learn that lesson early. We, the firm, are professionally responsible for all our clients, but we're not crusaders, we're corporate lawyers who do a few pro bono cases because... well, because DB insists. If I had my druthers... Oh, never mind! Do the research, file the bail application and then *I'll* decide what happens next." Avaristo picked up his red pen and tapped it against the glass desk. Grace took it as a signal to leave and lifted herself out of the chair. She had to move gingerly; the back of her head still throbbed and now her left leg was starting to feel stiff and painful as she limped back to her office to draft the bail application and to eat her banana.

4

It was a Saturday but Grace put on her work suit and jumped on a bus. Her plan was to find Willbess's home in Kalikiliki and interview his family. Avaristo did say that she should do research for the case. She checked her bag to confirm that she had everything she needed—a legal pad, her blue and red pens, and Willbess Mulenga's case file.

The first bus shuddered and honked its way to Cairo Road. Grace hopped off at Soweto Market and onto the next bus that lurched up the Great North Road, spewing passengers and black smoke along the way. The bus barely stopped long enough for Grace to jump out at the mouth of Kalikiliki, a sprawling township on the outskirts of the capital. From the Great North Road, she walked down a rutted dirt one and stopped at a group of women selling boiled groundnuts wrapped in newspaper cones. She showed them the address and they all pointed to the right, down a narrow path that threaded through endless rows of small, uniform houses.

The township was a world away from the suburb where Grace boarded with old Mrs. Njavwa in a small Cape Dutch–style bungalow. When she first arrived, Grace had never seen a house quite like it, with front gables curling ornately above the front door and sides of the building. The white paint was chipping, and there was no grass to speak of, but the tiny yard had an abundance of trees: a shaggy copse of bamboo next to the gate, several frangipani and a giant jacaranda that shielded the house from the afternoon sun. Grace hated the disorder of the townships—the cars, bicycles, men, women, children and animals all pressing through a maze of narrow paths. After fifteen minutes of walking and looking at the numbers painted on some of the houses, Grace realized that there was no discernible pattern. She stopped a shoeless boy to ask for directions. He agreed to take her there if she would give him two kwacha; she negotiated him down to one, and then followed him to the front of a neat house almost entirely hidden behind bougainvillea. A yellow dog appeared from under the hedge and barked aggressively from the front entrance—a large gap in the hedge. The boy took off without his money and Grace stood stock-still.

A man came out of the house. He was the color of river sand and too small for his suit. His jacket sloped off his shoulders, his sleeves covered most of his hands and his trousers draped over his shoes. Grace knew on sight that this was Willbess's father. He looked just like him, minus the swelling and bruising.

"I'm Grace Zulu, Willbess Mulenga's lawyer," Grace shouted over the barking.

The dog ignored the man's shushing and shooing until satisfied that its guard duties were done, and then wiggled back under the bougainvillea hedge. Willbess's father ushered her inside the house, where Grace found the whole family seated in a circle around a low table, sipping tea from large plastic mugs. They were dressed to go out, the women in matching chitenge and black plastic shoes.

"I'm Mr. Mulenga," the man said. "This is Mrs. Mulenga, the twins, Eneless and Agnes, and our youngest, Loveness."

Grace introduced herself again. The women all stood up and shook her hand formally. All the children looked like Mr. Mulenga. Mrs. Mulenga, in contrast, was almost as tall and dark as Grace. There were only five chairs so Loveness moved to let Grace sit. She noticed Mrs. Mulenga examining her and smoothed her skirt down to cover her knees. The living room was sparse, five dun-colored chairs covered in beige crochet doilies grouped around a wooden table squatting in the middle. The only bright color in the room was a framed picture hanging on the wall of a blond Jesus pointing to his very red, sacred heart. Loveness disappeared and reappeared with a porcelain cup filled to the brim with milky tea, with a biscuit balanced precariously on the saucer.

"We were just going to the prison. We've been there every day for weeks, and the police just keep telling us to come back tomorrow. Can you help us see our son?" Mr. Mulenga asked Grace.

"We don't have money for lawyers," Mrs. Mulenga interjected.

"My services are pro bono. I mean, free of charge," Grace responded, biting into the biscuit and washing it down with the tea. Hot, milky and sweet, just how she liked it. She noticed that they drank their tea without milk, and guessed there was probably no sugar either. In these times of shortages, she knew that she was being treated as an honored guest. She popped the rest of the biscuit in her mouth and blew on the hot tea before taking a few more noisy sips. "Thank you. This is excellent," she said to Loveness with appreciation. She had missed breakfast and was hungry.

"I've never heard of such a thing. What kind of a lawyer is free?" Mrs. Mulenga asked with open suspicion.

"Ba Mayo! Let her drink her tea before firing questions," Agnes said to her mother and Eneless nodded. Mr. Mulenga put his hand on his wife's before she could respond. She removed her hand from underneath his, crossed her arms and stuffed her fists into her armpits.

"It's a fair question." Grace looked into Mrs. Mulenga's unfriendly face and imagined how her round face and chubby cheeks might look jolly in happier times. "The firm that I work for, DB & Associates, normally charges, but we have a few special clients sent by Legal Aid whose costs are covered by the firm's profits."

"Can you take me to see my son now?" Mrs. Mulenga asked, sounding less aggressive than before.

"Unfortunately not right now, but I'll be filing a bail application on Monday to get him out as soon as possible."

"How long is as soon as possible?"

"It depends on the court giving us a hearing date, so it's hard to say, but I'm sure it'll be soon."

"Have you seen him?" Agnes asked.

"I saw him yesterday, very briefly."

"Is he okay?" both twins asked.

Grace hesitated. She didn't want to lie but she needed to get through her questions. She could only imagine their reaction if she told them what had happened at the prison, and what state Willbess was in.

"I know it's a difficult time and you have many questions, but if I may go first, I can get the answers I need to help your son's case, and then I'll do my best to answer you." She focused on Mr. Mulenga, who gave her a tight smile. Grace pulled out her legal pad and a pen, cleared her throat and began at the top of the list of questions, starting with standard formalities, confirmation of Willbess's full name and home address.

"You're here at the same address, aren't you?" Mrs. Mulenga answered. "My son's in trouble, and you are wasting time with stupid questions."

"Ba na Mpundu, she can't help us if you don't let her do her job," Mr. Mulenga pleaded.

"Her job? I don't think she knows what she is doing. How old is this girl anyway?" After an awkward pause, Grace continued, but skipped the next few routine questions.

"How old is Willbess?" She looked up and explained,

"Juvenile laws provide special protections if he's under eighteen."

"He's seventeen," the twins responded.

Grace was surprised that he was that old, he was so small. She quickly calculated that he had been born in 1973, the year when birth certificates had first became available in Zambia. "Do you have his birth certificate?" Grace asked hopefully. Most people didn't have one. She didn't.

Mr. Mulenga shook his head. "I wrote down his birthday, February 14, 1973, in my Bible. I recorded all my children's birthdays on the very day they were born. Loveness, bring the Bible from my bedside."

Loveness disappeared again. Grace wrote down the date and resisted the urge to bite her nails. A Bible wasn't a birth certificate, but if she could find some other corroborating evidence from his school, she might be able to get him released faster under *The Juveniles Act* that prohibited anyone under eighteen from being incarcerated with adults.

"Please tell me everything you know about the night of the alleged crime."

Agnes started talking and Eneless joined in, or was it the other way around? The twins had the same faces, voices, expressions and gestures.

"Bessy was just dancing," one twin said.

"Bessy?" Grace asked.

"That's what Willbess likes to be called."

"He insists!" the other twin added. Grace noticed Mrs. Mulenga frown.

"People clap and even pay him to dance. He dances very

well. They call him Zambian Janet Jackson because he's usually dressed up as a girl."

Mrs. Mulenga's head snapped in the direction of the twins, her face a storm. Grace wasn't sure if it was because the twins were revealing family secrets, or if she was hearing it for the first time. "We don't approve of such behavior," Mrs. Mulenga said. "Willbess has bad friends who take him to godforsaken places to drink alcohol and get into fights."

"He wasn't fighting!" the twins protested in unison.

One of them said, "We all share a room, so we heard him come in at about three in the morning." Mrs. Mulenga studied the bougainvillea hedge outside the window.

The other twin continued, "He made us all wake up to show us his latest dance routine, and told us about a big fight. He imitated the men throwing punches and falling down. We were all laughing."

"He said he ran away when the fight got out of control. Bessy would never fight, would he, Agnes?"

"No! People like to bother him and pick fights, but he won't hit back."

Grace made a mental note. It seemed that being beaten up was a common experience for Willbess.

"Loveness, do you know anything else?" Eneless turned to Loveness, who was standing in the doorway gripping a large Bible. Grace noticed that Loveness moved quickly to hand her the Bible before shaking her head. It's hard to lie with the good book in your hands. What are you hiding, Loveness? Grace wondered.

She opened the Bible and, as was the custom, she found the names and birthdays of all four of the Mulenga children written out neatly on the inside front page. Grace's father's Bible also had the names and birthdays of his six children— Joy, Innocence, Charity, Hope, Mercy and Grace—in her father's hand, and against five of them deathdays, all gone before they had reached the age of one. Only Grace had survived. She looked at the twins who sat joined at the hip, holding hands, and envied them. She liked to think that she would have been close to her siblings too, had they survived. Grace caressed the leather cover, fingered the worn and cracked corners and engraved gold cross. This had once been a fine Bible. She closed it, put it on the table and picked up her teacup. There was still a little tea left.

Mrs. Mulenga interrupted Grace's thoughts. "We don't know anything. We didn't even know he had gone out that night until the police arrested him early Sunday morning. No one tells us anything around here." She cut her eyes at her daughters.

"Did he resist arrest?"

"No!" the twins responded.

"Of course not. He's a respectful boy and went with the police immediately," Mrs. Mulenga added, corroborating Grace's belief that the police had beaten up Willbess while he was in custody.

Mr. Mulenga continued, "He said it was all a misunderstanding, he hadn't been involved in the bar fight and would be home by lunchtime. The police wouldn't let us go with him in their car, so we followed as soon as we could find a taxi, but by the time we got there he was already inside, and we haven't seen him since." Mr. Mulenga's eyes watered.

"Do you know anyone who might have been at the alleged crime scene?"

Mrs. Mulenga said hotly: "You just heard that he wasn't fighting, he was dancing. Since when is dancing a crime?"

Grace needed to clear up this misconception that Willbess had been arrested for fighting. She looked at the picture of Jesus and hesitated. She figured that they wouldn't take it too well but she had to tell them; it was their right to know, and she needed information that could help his case. Grace would be professional and matter-of-fact in her explanation of the law, and then resume her interview.

"Mrs. Mulenga, your son was charged with having sexual relations with another man."

Mrs. Mulenga reared up and shouted, "What? What are you saying about my son?"

Grace tried to reply. "I'm not saying—"

Mrs. Mulenga cut her off: "You dare enter my house and speak with a forked tongue to my God-fearing family?" She pointed a finger at Grace. "I rebuke thee, devil, I rebuke thee! Get out of my house!"

Grace's teacup rattled violently as she tried to put it down on the table. Mr. Mulenga shot out of his seat and stood between his wife and Grace.

"Get her out!" Mrs. Mulenga screeched at her husband. Agnes and Eneless each snatched an arm and ushered their mother out of the room. It was a small house so Grace could hear Mrs. Mulenga still screaming, "I want that demon out of my house!" while Mr. Mulenga shepherded Grace out of the front door.

Grace was shaken. Mrs. Mulenga had snapped without warning. "I wasn't accusing Willbess of anything, I was just trying to explain the charges," she said to Mr. Mulenga.

"My wife's very upset. They took our only boy from us and it's been a living hell ever since. We go to that prison every day, and she stays there all day, seven days a week. It will be five weeks tomorrow and they still won't let us see him. And now...now these vile accusations, these lies!" Mr. Mulenga kept shaking his head. "My son's a good boy, Ms. Zulu. Everyone who really knows him will tell you that he's a good boy."

Loveness and the yellow dog were waiting for Grace outside the bougainvillea hedge. She fell in step with Grace but stayed silent while the dog ran ahead, sniffing and squatting to pee every few meters.

"Is there something you want to tell me?" Grace finally prodded her silent escort.

"What'll happen to Bessy if he's convicted?" Loveness asked. Her voice was low and soft.

"Well, we are a long way away from worrying about a guilty verdict." Grace tried to be careful with her words. She was still shaken by Mrs. Mulenga's eruption. She hadn't done a good enough job of explaining that she wasn't accusing Willbess of anything, that it was a prosecutor who had reviewed the evidence and had decided the charges.

"But if it happened?" Loveness pressed.

"A judge would decide how much time he would serve in prison." Grace didn't mention that Willbess could serve fourteen years. "You have something to tell me?"

Loveness kicked a stone forward and kicked it again, but didn't answer.

"If I'm going to help your brother, you need to tell me everything you know."

Loveness lost the stone, but kept looking at her feet as she said, "Bessy likes dressing up as a girl." Grace knew that Willbess was wearing a dress when he was arrested, but he was an entertainer, and a dress could be part of the act and a non-prejudicial explanation for the court.

"That's not a crime."

"He likes boys," Loveness added even more quietly.

Grace stopped walking and looked hard at Loveness. From her expression, she knew what Loveness was saying. Grace realized that she had subconsciously gone beyond an objective legal presumption of innocence. Perhaps because he looked so young. She thought aloud: "Liking other boys isn't a crime either. Having sexual relations with another is, but the burden is on the prosecution to prove guilt beyond a reasonable doubt."

Loveness looked confused.

"Do you know anything else about that night at the Mac-Gyver?" Grace put her hand on Loveness's shoulder and as soon as she did, she heard a growl behind her. She hadn't realized that the dog had returned and was now glaring at her with angry hazel eyes. Grace took a step away from

Loveness. The last thing she needed was to be bitten by an overprotective hound.

"Munali! Home! Go home!" Loveness shouted and the dog immediately took off at full speed back in the direction of the house. "She's Bessy's dog. He trained her himself," Loveness said, watching the dog sprint away. Grace wondered why a yellow dog would be called Munali, "the Red One."

"Did Willbess have any friends at the bar?" Grace asked. She was running out of time before the next minibus, and so far she had nothing that would help her client. Loveness shook her head.

"No one I know. Well, maybe. There was a boy who came home once when my parents were away in Kasama for a funeral. He and Bessy both wore dresses and wigs and practiced a dance routine to do together at the MacGyver. His name is Godfredah. Maybe his real name is Fred. I don't know."

"How do I get to the MacGyver Bar?"

"You can't go there."

"Why not?"

"The MacGyver is for men. Men only, you understand?"

A gay bar in Lusaka? How was that possible in conservative Zambia? She handed Loveness her legal pad. "Draw me a map."

"Once I followed Bessy there and tried to go in but the bouncer told me to *voetsek*. He said he'd snap my neck if I ever came back."

"A map, please."

"That bouncer won't let you in," Loveness warned again but took the legal pad, balanced it on one knee and drew a map.

Grace traced the arrows Loveness had drawn, from where they stood just before the Great North Road to an X marking the MacGyver. She looked back up the dusty road and replied mostly to herself, "I'll find a way. I always do."

Nyamphande Village

1985

5

The sun was still low in the sky but already dazzling and hot. Grace was pounding dried maize into meal. She had found her rhythm, lifting the heavy pestle high in the air and then crashing down into the mortar with a grunt, again and again, pulverizing the kernels. As she pounded, Grace was thinking about the previous Sunday when she had enjoyed a rare, quiet morning by the river doing nothing but watching bee-eaters exiting their nests in the riverbank to catch insects over the water. She had pretended to be sick a few times already and was trying to think of a new excuse, when her anyina appeared in her peripheral vision. Her mother's sudden appearance made Grace feel like just by thinking about her, she had conjured her up. Anyina waved at Grace to stop and so she brought the pestle down, slowly this time, held it balanced in the mortar with one hand and wiped her brow with the back of the other. "Morning, Anyina, I'm almost done and won't be late for church."

Shamu! Without a good excuse ready, she capitulated without a fight. It was easier to endure church for a few hours than to fight all week with her mother about not going.

"No church for you today. I need you to go to the market and buy yourself a new dress for the wedding. I've arranged for you to marry the Chief."

Grace let go of the pestle and the mortar tipped over, projecting kernels and maize meal into the dust.

"Leave that!" her mother shouted at Grace, who had fallen on her knees to rescue the spilled maize and try to make sense of what her mother had said. It was the first time Grace had heard anything about getting married, much less to the Chief.

"But I can't get married, I'm going to university," was all Grace managed to say. She felt unsteady as she got back on to her feet.

"I don't want to hear about more school!" her mother erupted. "You've already had too much school and it's only made you more stupid and stubborn." Chickens appeared from nowhere and started pecking at the kernels in the dust. Anyina kicked at them until they scattered. "Do you have *any* idea what I had to go through to arrange this marriage? I had to convince the Chief that you've been cured of njilinjili, praise Jesus, you no longer have seizures! And I had to assure him that you'll be an obedient wife despite your schooling. So you need to stop acting like you are cleverer than everyone else."

Do you have any idea what I had to go through to stay in school? Grace thought but didn't say. The lonely years as the only girl left after all the others dropped out to get married. How hard it was to study and stayed focused with the constant taunting, bullying and harassment. How it was even worse after her father died and the boys thought that there would be no consequences. Grace had to fight to defend herself, punching and kicking the boys who grabbed her breasts, or pulled up her skirt. How her dream of university had sustained her through it all and now, after all of her struggles, she would end up even worse off than the others—married to a man old enough to be her grandfather.

"I've an acceptance letter from the university and I'm going. Atate always said so."

"Atate? Don't you dare mention him. Your father died and left us with nothing. Worse than nothing, he—" Her mother stopped herself. Grace could see her reconsider her tactics as she shifted her weight from one bare foot to the other. She sighed and then spoke again in a softer tone: "Your father is gone and now you're a grown woman so it's time to put aside the childish ideas he put in your head. Marrying well is our last chance at a good life, Grace. Do you want to keep scratching in the dirt like a chicken forever? We barely have enough to eat as it is, how could you think that we'd have money for university?"

Grace had assumed that the village would pool their money as they had for Tiloleko, the last boy from the village to make it to university a few years back. If Grace was betrothed to the Chief, she knew that no such arrangements would be possible for her.

"I'm not marrying that old goat."

Her mother slapped her. Since her father died, her mother had become even more angry and aggressive, hitting her frequently. She was a petite, wiry woman whose slaps hurt Grace's feelings more than inflicting much physical pain. "You'll do as you're told. Take this money and buy a dress for the wedding feast." Her mother thrust a twenty kwacha note into Grace's hand. Even as Grace threw the money into the dust in defiance, her heart sank; for her mother to have this kind of money meant that the bride price had been paid and the deal sealed. As far back as Grace could remember, her father had said that her destiny was different from the other girls in the village, that she was going to the University of Zambia—the only one in the country—to study law. It was true that her mother had never said much when they had talked about university, but she had never voiced any opposition either, and she had never said anything about her getting married. Grace felt an overwhelming urge to punch her mother in the face and keep punching until all those sharp angles were reduced to mush. She clenched her fist but then froze. Her mother sucked her teeth, as if daring Grace to strike her, then turned her back on her daughter and strolled in the direction of the village church. "Buy something blue," she called over her shoulder. "The Chief wants you in a blue dress."

Grace unclenched her fist. As soon as her anyina was out

of sight, Grace ducked into their hut and packed all her possessions. In the center of a chitenge she laid her grey church
dress, the brown blouse and the black skirt that was her old
school uniform, her once white t-shirt, her flip-flops, some
chewing sticks, a square of carbolic soap and her father's
Bible with her university acceptance letter tucked between
the pages. She pulled the corners of the fabric together and
tied everything into a tight bundle. She stamped her feet
into her canvas shoes and left immediately, pausing only
to swoop down and pick up the twenty kwacha, blow off
the dust and place it safely in her bra.

Most of the village would be in church, but she took
the long way along the river to be sure that no one would
see her leave. Grace had a rough map in her mind—follow
the bank of the Nyakawise until the fork in the river, turn
north to join the dirt road to Mr. Patel's shop and then catch
a bus west to Lusaka. Her plan was made in haste and was
hazy in most places, but it had to work, she would will it
to work. As she walked farther and farther along the river,
questions started to swarm her mind. What if Mr. Patel
won't help me? What if the Chief sends his men to drag
me back? What will Anyina do to me? Grace was tired and
both of her arms ached despite swapping the bundle from
one shoulder to the other. She placed it down on the ground
and rested on her haunches. The questions played on a loop
in her brain until panic seized her whole body. It's not too
late to go back now, she thought, but she couldn't will her
body to move backwards. She realized that she was under

a msolo tree, so she lay down in the dust and tried to summon her ancestors.

They said that the msolo tree was sacred, that the ancestors favored its thick canopy to watch the villagers unseen and to whisper to each other. Sometimes ngangas would stand under the trees with their charms, amulets and crowns of beads and feathers, and translate the whispers, usually warnings that the ancestors were angry and that punishment in the form of locusts, drought or floods was imminent. Sometimes no nganga was needed to translate the whispers, like when an unknown culprit turned a copse of msolo trees into charcoal. Furious, the ancestors sent floods so bad that they unburied the dead in the village cemetery. Grace knew when they were close—the ndembo on her face and back warmed and she would feel more powerful and courageous—but she couldn't seem to summon them. Only ngangas had that power; for her, they seemed to come and go as they pleased, oblivious to her earthly troubles. She tried to call her father. She hadn't felt him since his funeral. Surely becoming an ancestor didn't mean you forgot your own children. Atate, please help! she implored and then listened and looked hard, but heard nothing more than rustling leaves and saw nothing more than the tree's canopy, a pale sky and wispy clouds delicate as lace drifting high above. She struggled not to lose hope and the courage that had gotten her this far.

A splash behind her woke her up. She hadn't realized that she had fallen asleep, and without thinking, jerked up and scrambled on her hands and knees behind the tree.

Mr. Mambilima punted past her using a long bamboo pole to navigate his canoe full of silver, thrashing fish back to the village for his wife, Kaya, to sell in the market. Kaya had been Grace's classmate before she left primary school to marry and, as was the custom, was now called Anyina Chisoni after her first-born child. In school, Grace and Kaya had vied to be the teacher's pet, both waving to answer every question, but now she was Anyina Chisoni, waving at the flies settling on her dried fish and her three children playing in the dust around her market stall. Grace's anyina would haggle endlessly and complain about the shameless price-gouging going on in the market, but it was particularly embarrassing in front of Anyina Chisoni and her children.

Grace pressed her back into the tree. That wasn't going to be her fate, she promised herself. If Mr. Patel couldn't help her get to university, she would come back to this serene spot, wade into the water and swim to where the river swirled and churned, and slip under the surface forever to join her father and siblings. Grace knew that death was never that easy, but the option made her feel powerful, in control of her life, and as if the spell her mother had over her was broken. She didn't have to do what her mother wanted anymore. Why had she ever felt that she had to?

"What can my anyina do to me? Nothing!" Grace shouted after Mr. Mambilima, but he seemed not to hear her, at least he didn't look back before he disappeared around a bend in the river.

★ ★ ★

Grace had visited Mr. Patel's store almost every weekend with her father. Then, it was a two-story wooden box with a wraparound veranda. "Mr. Patel & Sons General Store" was written in bright, bold letters on the building's gable. Mr. Patel sold everything—mealie-meal, beans, dried fish, cooking oil, sugar, chitenge, overalls, boots, fertilizer, pesticides—and on Sundays he turned his veranda into a restaurant. Childless himself, he was one of the four "& Sons" of the late, original Mr. K. P. Patel. As a young girl, Grace had been intrigued by the "& Sons" always freshly painted in some bright color. She would ask Mr. Patel, "What are your brothers' names? Where do they live? When was the last time you saw them?"

"I already told you their names. I think they're still in Chipata. I haven't seen them in a long, long time."

"Why?" At the age of six, her favorite question.

Mr. Patel would wipe away tears and say something to the effect that keeping the store instead of selling it, like most things he did, was against his brothers' wishes.

"You should tell them that it's everyone's favorite shop."

"You mean it's the *only* shop!" Grace's father would laugh, long and deep with his head thrown back, before changing the subject. But later, hitching a ride home on the back of an ox-cart laden with fertilizer, he would remind Grace not to pester Mr. Patel about his brothers.

She remembered one time pressing her father: "But why?"

"Because it makes him sad and, before you ask why

again, his brothers find it hard to love him because he's different from them."

"But aren't Mr. Patel's brothers Indians too?"

Her father smiled. "Yes they are, but there are other reasons that you'll understand better when you're older. His brothers have turned their backs on him, so you and me are his family. Now remember, we stick together no matter what. Promise me that you'll never be like Mr. Patel's brothers."

Grace nodded and felt that she understood. "I won't be like them, or my anyina."

"Oh, Grace! Your mother's trying to protect you. A woman's life isn't easy and she's preparing you, making you tough. It's not her way to show it, but she does love you. And I love you too, more than anything and anyone in this world. You know that, right?" He pulled her close until Grace started to squirm. "Look! What's this?" Her father pretended to pull sweets out of her ear. It was the same every time. Mr. Patel would claim that he had no sweets for her, and then her father would magically produce them on the long ride home. Even when she was older and could have grabbed them out of his sleeves, Grace would wait for him to perform his magic trick.

Grace had seen Mr. Patel only once since her father died. Soon after the funeral, he had brought her and her mother mealie-meal, cooking oil and sugar, but before he had had time to unload the back of his van, her mother chased him away like one of the scrawny yellow village dogs that belonged to no one. She had shouted in Mr. Patel's face, "You brought your filthy disease to this village and now you think you can buy me with a bag of mealie-meal? You killed Atate Grace! Murderer! *Voetsek!*"

It didn't make sense to Grace. Why would her anyina blame Mr. Patel? The mines killed him. Black lung—her mother had said so herself. If anything, Mr. Patel had tried to convince her father not to go to the mines. A farmer can't survive in a dark hole all day without the sun, he had said.

Mr. Patel's face contorted at the word "murderer," but before he retreated into his van he said to her anyina, "We were best friends since childhood, nothing more and nothing less."

"Muthanyula!" her mother spat back at him before he drove away. Grace had known that Mr. Patel was different long before that moment, but to hear her religious mother use a vile slur was a shock.

At the church service the following Sunday, her mother interrupted the priest before he could begin his sermon. She had an important message for the congregation from Jesus. Grace sank lower on the bench. It wasn't the first time that her mother claimed to be a prophet with a message from Jesus, the Holy Spirit, or from God himself. Grace found it preposterous, but most people in the village seemed to take her seriously and listened intently. Her mother stood before the altar, a simple wooden table, in front of the small church, right on the spot where light shafted through the only window, so that her whole body appeared haloed.

"The Lord came to me last night in a dream to warn

me of an evil spirit. A demon close by." The other villagers murmured and looked around. "Jesus said to me, 'Anyina Grace, can't you see him? A profiteer who gets richer, as you get poorer. Gets fatter, as you get thinner. A man with no wife and no family. A man who rejects me as his Lord and savior!'" Grace's mother lifted up her hands to the heavens and shouted, "This man is the devil's host, bringing disease and death to our village." She spun around a few times and then fell to the ground and began to growl, "Cast out Lucifer. Exorcise him with fire." She crawled across the mud floor to the mukwa cross adorning the front wall of the church, where she stayed on her knees muttering about fire, before roaring up and speaking in tongues.

Grace couldn't endure another one of her mother's performances and crept out of the church to sun herself on the boulders by the river.

She didn't hear her mother come into their hut late that night, and in the morning, as was her custom to avoid arguments about school, Grace left before the sun and her anyina rose. At school, she found that everyone was talking about what had happened after church. They told Grace that half the congregation had marched all the way to Mr. Patel's, hog-tied him and burned his store to the ground. The boys even re-enacted the scene with one boy as her anyina, speaking in tongues and making the sign of the cross over a second boy, who was supposed to be Mr. Patel. This boy lay curled on the ground with his hands behind his back, pleading in Nsenga and nonsense Hindi until the first boy proceeded to kick and gag him. An internal riptide of horror and shame almost brought Grace to her knees. She sat at her desk before she fell down; she drew in deep breaths and swallowed hard several times to stop herself from vomiting. When her teacher started the lesson, Grace couldn't follow what he was saying, or decipher what looked like hieroglyphics on the chalkboard. She couldn't understand anything. How could her anyina have done this to Mr. Patel, and how could anyone else go along with such madness? Grace's confusion and anger dissolved into guilt for leaving church early. Maybe she could have stopped it—not that her mother would have listened to her, but the rest of the villagers might have listened to reason.

Grace planned to confront her mother when she got home, but when her anyina began screaming at her for not refilling the calabashes with water, she lost her nerve. She would do it when she got back from the well, and then the next day after school, and then the next week, month and then never. There was never a good time to confront her anyina; her mother was volatile enough without provocation. When it came to her mother, Grace lost her courage and felt overwhelmed with fear. That Grace never confronted her mother haunted her. She understood what her father had asked of her so many years ago; that when she grew up, she didn't turn her back on Mr. Patel. But by not speaking up, not raising it at all with her mother, or the church, Grace was no better than Mr. Patel's brothers. That Mr. Patel had rebuilt his store did little to assuage her guilt for not standing up for him when it mattered. She felt she was not the daughter her father taught her to be, and she wasn't the person she wanted to be.

It took Grace much longer than she had thought to walk the distance from the river to Mr. Patel's store. The new building looked like the old one, a two-story box with a wraparound veranda, but this one was slightly bigger and built with concrete, not wood. It was Sunday so the restaurant was open. More accurately, Mr. Patel had placed a few tables and chairs on the veranda and propped up a sign which read "Prix fix: 3 kwacha = 1 spicy vegetarian samosas (main), 1 bananas (dessert); 1 Fanta (beverage). No Cokes. No Exchanges. No Refunds."

Grace watched Mr. Patel steadily thumping the back of the only patron, who was coughing violently over a half-eaten samosa. "Don't complain, spices cure gases, bloating and constipations."

A black cat rushed out of the store and greeted Grace, rubbing herself against Grace's legs. "Hello, Priyanka," she said. On hearing Grace's voice, Mr. Patel abandoned the man and also rushed to her.

"My little Gracie!" He had always called her that, even though she had grown taller than him many years ago, and now stood a head above him. She hadn't been sure what reception she would receive; she'd been too ashamed to visit since her mother had burned down his shop, and felt intensely relieved at Mr. Patel's welcome. He had aged and become thinner in the years since she last saw him. She felt the knobs of his backbone through the thin material of his kurta, and although his hair was still thick, it was now more grey than black. Mr. Patel held on long after Grace let go. When he finally released her, he sat her down, placed her bundle on a spare chair, then dashed inside to find her some food. As the fear and tension of the day left her body, she felt more exhausted than hungry. She leaned back in her chair, closed her eyes and inhaled deeply.

The sweet and sour smells of turmeric, cloves, coriander and nutmeg that hung in the air around Mr. Patel's store brought back memories of her father. He liked to sit on the low wall that ran only on the left side of the otherwise open veranda, smoking after a heavy meal. If she was quiet, and especially if they were drinking, they would forget she was there and the two men would talk freely. In this way she learned that her father had been abandoned as a young boy with Cold Old Patel, as they called Mr. Patel's father; that Mrs. Patel had died giving birth to Mr. Patel and Cold Old Patel hated him even before he realized his son was different; that her father was a child servant, but the two boys did all the housework together so that they would have time to play; and that once he was a teenager, Cold Old Patel threw her father out of the house. The story was murky but Grace pieced together that it had something to do with saving his friend from a bad whipping and threatening Cold Old with the same belt. The two men would joke about the horrors of growing up but it was her father's nature to find a silver lining. "I was lucky he threw me out, otherwise I'd have never moved to Nyamphande, met my wife and had you, Gracie, my miracle." She opened her eyes, half expecting to see him there with his long legs stretched out and the big smile he had on his face when about to tell her a funny story. He had always said that Grace was far too serious for a child and had tried hard to make her laugh.

Her appetite returned as soon as Mr. Patel placed a pile of samosas and a Fanta in front of her. "Had I known you were coming, I would've cooked dal, bhindi, chapatis and rice for you. Remember when you were young you used to like helping me in the kitchen chopping vegetables and grinding spices?" Grace nodded but kept on chewing and throwing one crispy triangle after another into her mouth in quick succession. Priyanka jumped onto Mr. Patel's lap and Grace felt the two sets of large eyes watching her as she ate. Mr. Patel's flickered with worry, while the cat's green eyes darted back and forth following each samosa from the plate to Grace's mouth.

"Priya, why are you acting like you didn't just have lunch?" Mr. Patel scolded gently as he lifted a samosa off the pile and gave it to his cat. Priya leapt down, landing without a sound, and walked majestically back into the store with the prize between her teeth.

"I don't think samosas are good for cats," Grace said before stuffing another crispy triangle into her mouth.

"Nonsense! Spices are good for both mens and beasts. Priya will tell you that she's never had a day of constipations." Mr. Patel always added an S to words indiscriminately when he spoke English, which he insisted on doing with Grace so that she could practice for university.

When she finished eating, Grace drained her Fanta and

then sat back feeling restored, almost as if her ordeal had happened to someone else. Mr. Patel eyed her bundle and asked, "Now tell me, my little Gracie, what's going on?"

Her feelings rushed back in full force. How could she explain it all? She blurted out, "My mother arranged for me to marry the Chief."

"No, no, no!" Mr. Patel stood up, put his hands on his head and began pacing.

"I told her that I'm not getting married, I'm going to university—" Grace touched her left cheek "—and she hit me. Again."

Mr. Patel stopped pacing, sat back down and moved his chair closer. "We'll talk to the Chief. He's a reasonable man, and he certainly doesn't need a fourth wife."

Grace tried to be discreet in retrieving the money from her bra, and then opened her palm to show Mr. Patel the twenty kwacha that her mother had given her. "It's from the bride price. Anyina gave it to me to buy a dress for the wedding feast."

Mr. Patel stared at the money and began to cry. He took several minutes before he wiped away tears on the sleeves of his kurta. Unlike Grace, Mr. Patel's emotions were always on display.

"Twenty kwacha isn't enough for university," she said. She knew that she was stating the obvious, but wasn't sure how else to ask for money. Mr. Patel's store barely turned a profit, she had heard him and her father lament their bad fortunes often enough on this very veranda, but she had no one else to turn to.

"Don't you worry, my little Gracie, tomorrow you'll be leaving here with monies for university, a one-way ticket and enough samosas to feed the whole bus." Mr. Patel ushered her upstairs to the door of his flat above the store, and then rushed back down to lock up the shop.

Grace waited at the door for Mr. Patel, who ran back up and paused, slightly out of breath. "Go in, go in. Make yourself at home." The sun had set and the room was completely dark. He felt along the wall and switched on the light, revealing a concrete square made attractive with bright rugs, cushions and saris draped over the windows. Grace took off her shoes and entered with her mouth open. Mr. Patel's old flat had been sparse and utilitarian. She remembered it as a spare room with a metal-framed double bed, a mukwa desk and closet set, and reed mats both on the floor and hanging unevenly over the windows. Even when the window mats were tied up in a roll, little light seemed able to penetrate the glass to brighten the drab square. This space was the opposite; the fluorescent lights set the rug, cushions and curtains ablaze with color. Grace touched the green silk with gold brocade trim that he had draped artfully over the windows.

"Those were my mother's saris. I got everything here from Vivek's house. Do you remember my oldest brother, Vivek?"

Grace nodded. Even though she couldn't quite picture his face, she remembered the strong, negative feelings she had for all Mr. Patel's brothers.

"These saris have been in storage since she died. First

by my father and then by Vivek. They are so beautiful, why should they stay hidden in a trunk full of mothballs. My brother has dementia now. Shamu, shamu!" Mr. Patel shook his head for a long time. "He's forgotten everything, including how much he hates me, and now he's as sweet and loving as a child. His wife says that's the one silver lining of his awful disease. Just imagine how wonderful, she invited me to stay with them in Chipata while the store was being rebuilt after the fire." At the mention of the fire, Grace felt her stomach knot, but Mr. Patel continued walking and talking. "Their children are all in Lusaka so she was happy to have my help." He beckoned her into a large bathroom. "Look, I have indoor plumbings now." He flushed the toilet to show her how it worked and twisted the taps above a big tub with feet like an animal. "Feel this." He knelt down and pulled Grace's hand under the running water. She jerked her hand back, surprised that it was hot, and they both laughed. She followed him to a more austere bedroom and Mr. Patel lifted the pillow, removed the case and pulled off the sheets. Wrapping everything but the blanket into a bundle, he left the room and told Grace to get fresh sheets from the closet. The closet door panels hung loose on their hinges and caught on each other, but she managed to arrange them just so to pull them open. Inside, she found a few kurtas hanging on wire frames, a black suit on a wooden hanger, a few white shirts folded neatly on one shelf, two pairs of trousers on the next down, and on the bottom shelf, two colorful striped towels and the sheets she was looking for. Under the closet were a pair of slippers, identical to the ones Mr. Patel had on his feet, and one pair of brown lace-ups that looked new and unworn.

They made the bed together. Mr. Patel floated and snapped each sheet and then Grace placed the blanket on top, tucking it under the mattress until everything was flat and tight as Mr. Patel instructed. He struggled with the pillow until it was stuffed into a case that was too small and placed it on the bed, then, carefully opening the closet so that the doors didn't catch, took one of the towels out. A minute later, Grace could hear running water. Mr. Patel called, "Come, Gracie. Have a long hot bath and then sleep in my bed. Mind Priyanka, she has a habit of jumping on your head in the middle of the night. The kitchen is still outside in the yard, but there are Fantas and samosas in the icebox." He pointed through the bathroom door to a white metal box in the corner of the main room. "Pull the silver handle to open the icebox and make sure to close it properly, otherwise the cold will escape. Priya will beg for samosas but don't give her more than one or two. Four samosas at the utmost."

Mr. Patel lifted a bunch of keys from a bowl on his desk. He wrestled with it until he had twisted his car key off the ring and handed the rest to Grace. "Follow me and lock the store behind me with this—" he showed her a big iron key "—and for the door to this flat, use the smaller copper one." He showed her both keys again and Grace nodded. "Don't open these doors for anyone until I get back." He hugged her quickly and left.

From the other side of the front door as she locked it,

Grace heard Mr. Patel's van door slam and then the engine rev and rattle. Back in the flat, she rushed to the window and caught a glimpse of his taillights before they disappeared into the dark night.

There was no moon, stars or light from any of the surrounding villages, and she could hear no noise either. She wondered how Mr. Patel could live in this no-man's-land between villages. Moonless nights like this were just as dark in the village, but it was never quiet. Every night, it seemed, Mr. and Mrs. N'dlovu either argued or made love equally noisily; Anyina Chisoni's colicky baby cried; the frogs by the river croaked; and the yellow dogs howled for the missing moon and the wind carried their complaint far and wide—but not this far. Grace found the silence disquieting. To her relief, Priya began yowling in front of the icebox. Grace opened up the fridge, extracted two samosas and gave them both to the cat. Too exhausted to eat herself, she left Priya devouring the samosas to take a bath. The water was cold so she pulled out the plug, drained some of the water and twisted the hot tap on. When the tub was full, she stepped out of her dusty clothes and eased herself into the steam. For her last hot bath, she had had to collect the firewood, boil big pots of water on braziers and carefully pour the boiling water into a tin tub. That tub was shallow and the water not hot for long—not worth the trouble, to Grace's mind, but her anyina insisted that she take a full bath for church holidays, especially Easter and Christmas. On these occasions, instead of a basin of water, or a dunk in the river, the whole village became preoccupied with preparing their hot baths, and scrubbing themselves from head to toe with carbolic soap and stones from the river. It was a different experience lying in a deep tub full of hot water, with the warmth penetrating her skin, flesh, muscles until even her bones felt pliant and she had no other choice but to relax. Grace's anxieties about her mother, the Chief and money for university leached out of her and seemed to be lifted away by the rising steam. After a few minutes, she found herself preoccupied with the mechanics of plumbing instead. Where did the water come from? Where did it go? How did it come out hot? Grace used a foot to push the hot water tap on once more, and used her hands like fins to even out the temperature of the waters enveloping her. She kept falling asleep in the tub, so eventually dragged herself out, barely dried herself, and fell into Mr. Patel's soft bed. Realizing the mattress was far shorter than the two reed mats she usually slept on, she curled up like the cat next to her and fell asleep.

The next day, Grace woke up to the sound of knocking downstairs and unfamiliar voices calling for Mr. Patel. Her momentary disorientation was replaced with fear and her heart began to thrash in her chest like a newly caged bird. She crept to the window and looked down from behind the curtain but couldn't see the men whose voices drifted up from the veranda below. She could hear two men talking about Mr. Patel and if he was opening the shop or not. Mr. Patel's van was gone, one remarked; but there's no notice, replied the other. He would leave a note if he wasn't

opening. Soon their voices grew more agitated and they
seemed to egg each other on. They complained that Mr.
Patel was inconsiderate and selfish for disappearing without notice; that he was greedy and grasping and his prices
were too high; and that KK should've kicked him out in
the seventies when he expelled the other no-good Indians. Finally, with a few bangs of frustration, they gave up
and Grace watched them leave. She hated their narrow
backs and wished Mr. Patel would return and run them
over with his van.

Priya sat before the locked door to the flat and began
yowling again. Grace used the small copper key to open it,
then followed the cat downstairs into the store, but without
the front doors open it felt like a dark cavern full of omi-
nous shapes. While she felt foolish being afraid of shadows,
Grace still fled back upstairs. As she washed her face, she
noticed that she had left a thick, dirty ring in the bathtub
the night before so rubbed the scum away with an old piece
of chitenge and scouring powder that she found under the
sink. She then used the same rag to clean the floor, careful to collect all the dust that her clothes had deposited the
night before. When she was done, she washed the chitenge
scrap in the sink and hung it on the side of the tub to dry.
When the bathroom was spotless, she went to the bedroom
to make the bed as Mr. Patel had shown her. Grace wanted
him to find the place just as neat and clean as he had left it.

Satisfied with her cleaning job, she put a chewing stick
in her mouth and bit and sucked it as she did another tour
of the flat. It seemed bigger in the soft morning light and

she admired the details that she hadn't noticed the previous night. The cushions had humming birds embroidered into thread forests; the saris caught the sunlight like fish nets; and the individual pieces of the parquet floor showed off the patina of their previous lives as trees. She picked up a book and then realized that it was in Hindi, not that she could focus enough to read anyway. She took a Fanta from the icebox and began her vigil for Mr. Patel, standing a step behind the window where she could see without being seen.

By late morning, there were throngs of people using the crossroads in front of Mr. Patel & Sons. Women carried firewood on their heads, boys herded goats, men guided laden ox-carts and one bus painted in the colors of the national flag—black, green, red and copper—raced past leaving a wake of spinning dust. Grace worried that she had missed the bus to Lusaka but told herself that this one was going east, perhaps as far as Mozambique. She remembered her father had given her a map of Zambia his first trip home from the mines. Nyamphande wasn't on the map so he had traced his journey from the nearest town, Petauke, west to Lusaka, and there a change of bus to go north to the Copperbelt. He had tapped a circle labeled Kitwe, the mining town where he lived and worked most of the year. She loved looking at the map, exploring the whole country with her fingers, and tracing the roads and rivers into neighboring countries—Malawi, Mozambique, Zimbabwe, Botswana, Namibia, Angola, Tanzania and Zaire—names that floated around Zambia's borders but countries that weren't otherwise drawn on this map. She would often sit by the Nyaka-wise river and imagine paddling a canoe to the Zambezi, and then all the way to the end, where she had learned in school that the river became an ocean.

The sun said midday when Grace finally saw Mr. Patel appear on the dirt road walking swiftly towards the store. She ran downstairs with the keys jangling in her hand and fumbled with the big iron key until it clicked and she could pull open the door. Mr. Patel showed Grace an envelope stuffed with kwacha. "Look!" he said, laughing and hugging her.

"Where's the van? Did you sell your van?" Grace kept asking Mr. Patel as she followed him upstairs. He grabbed two Fantas and beckoned her to join him sitting cross-legged on a cushion on the floor.

"Nothing to worry about, my van is collateral, I'll get it back soon. Now, a toast!"

Grace sat down and clinked bottles with Mr. Patel. She felt terrible but as soon as he handed her the envelope, she got up to put it away inside her father's Bible next to her university acceptance letter. She then hid the bulging Bible inside the folds of her grey church dress and retied the bundle. She returned to the same spot, careful not to knock over her Fanta. "I'll pay you back as soon as I can," she promised.

Mr. Patel waved his hand as if swatting a fly. "It's a gift, in memory of my best friend, my *only* friend, as he would joke." Mr. Patel began to weep again. "But it was true, your father was my singular friend. Always defending me from the time we were boys, always there through life's thicks and thins. You share your father's instinct to defend people. You're so much like him."

Grace shook her head. She wasn't good or strong or brave like her father, and feeling overwhelmed with guilt, blurted out, "I was in church that morning when my anyina planned to burn down your store. But I didn't understand what she was talking about, I promise. I never thought that she could do anything so—" Grace thought about her own predicament "—evil. I'm sorry. Please forgive me."

"What could you have done, my Gracie? There were so many of them that day. Your mother has always hated me, but the others…" Mr. Patel grimaced. "I thought they were my friends. Anyway the story has a happy ending. With the insurance moneys, I built an even better store, and just look at my flat." His dainty hands darted around like little birds as he talked again about the indoor plumbing, and the new mukwa shelving in his store that was strong enough to hold ten-liter tins of cooking oil, sacks of mealie-meal, pallets of sugar and even bags of fertilizer. "And almost all of my customers are back. Who else would give them credits?" Mr. Patel laughed but his eyes looked sad. "I've been worried about you too, but now I can see that I shouldn't have been. Your father would be so proud of you." He clapped his hands and then clasped them together as if in prayer and said, "Atate Grace, we did it! Our beloved child is going to university!"

Lusaka

November 1990

6

Suzanna, Grace's friend and former roommate from university, was driving the sleek maroon Mercedes down a patchwork of dirt, tar and potholes. They were unlikely friends, opposites in both body and temperament. Suzanna was short and plump with light-brown skin, and wore her hair in long thin blond braids that snaked down her back all the way to her waist. She was as loquacious and over-confident as only someone born into money could be.

The car made a cracking noise as Suzanna hit another pothole. "Shit! If I put a dent in my dad's Benzie, he'll put a dent in my head. He doesn't know we borrowed it."

"We? You mean you. I wanted to take a taxi." Grace worried about damaging the car, she worried about her half-baked plan to find Godfredah and she worried about the cost of this night out—she had her last 100 kwacha tucked in her bra, and it would be another two long weeks before payday. She hoped she wouldn't have to spend too much. The free ride helped, but she didn't want to rely on Suzanna for money, even if her friend threw kwacha around like maize kernels.

"We're supposed to be rich bitches looking for exotic entertainment. Who's going to be impressed if we arrive in a batty old taxi?" Suzanna pulled the steering wheel wildly to the left and then back to the right to avoid hitting another pothole. Grace braced herself by gripping the dashboard. "Is this MacGyver place really a gay club? I can't wait to tell the Londoners!" Suzanna said, referring to her trio of friends who went to university in London. Grace didn't get why she was so enamored of them. They made it clear that because they had more money, they were superior, and that going to the University of Zambia was something that "poor Nana" should be ashamed of. It was Grace's first inkling that there were levels of rich people. She couldn't abide them and their condescending attitude, and their boring and superficial conversations that never seemed to go beyond nightclubs and pop stars. It would start with Suzanna insisting that Prince was the best musician of all time as she danced to his music, pausing only to flip the cassette and kiss her poster of a pretty man sitting on a giant purple motorbike; then Birdie would made the case for Michael Jackson with Brads agreeing; and Dickie would get shouted down for suggesting Madonna. On and on for hours. Worst of all, Suzanna changed in their presence, rolling her eyes whenever Grace spoke, whispering to Birdie, and not inviting her when they went out. The few times she did go with them, it was at Brads's insistence, and each time she regretted it. The elegant home, restaurant or nightclub made her feel more like a misfit than ever—an alien in this world of posh terrestrials. They had taught her that word, "posh," referring mainly to themselves. Worst of all, in their presence "Nana" made Grace feel like a trespasser in her own room instead of the best friends she proclaimed them to be when the Londoners weren't around.

"I can't believe this club really exists in this boring town. Tonight's going to be coolio!" Grace was glad for Suzanna's enthusiasm, it helped tamp down her own worries and doubts.

They heard the soukous music before they arrived at the bar. The Zairean singer Franco crooned languidly in Lingala and French while his OK Jazz band blew trumpets, thumbed electric guitars and beat drums with wild energy. There was no sign, but several cars surrounded an unassuming grey box of a building with one visible door. Insects swirled in the light above the door and over the head of a tall, obese bouncer in a tight white t-shirt with a Union Jack emblazoned across his chest and round belly.

"There! There's a good parking spot right where the bouncer can see us." Grace jabbed at the air in front of Suzanna's face. Suzanna swatted her hand out of the way, stopped suddenly and reversed fast and expertly into the spot, revving and spinning up gravel and dust. Taxi drivers leaning against their dilapidated cars, sucking hand-rolled cigarettes and tapping their feet to the music, raised their heads briefly and then looked down again. This wasn't a place for looking too hard.

"Loveness said that the bouncer might not let us in," Grace added, feeling even less confident now that they were outside the bar.

"What would Lovey, or whatever her name is, know? Fifty kwacha *always* works." Suzanna pulled some notes out of her purple clutch bag. She adjusted her bra and undid one more button of her purple shirt to reveal non-existent cleavage. "I think we look hot tonight, don't you?"

Grace looked down at her borrowed outfit. It was a stretchy, boob-tube dress that was too long on Suzanna but still too short for Grace. It was purple, as were almost all of Suzanna's possessions, and Grace really hated it, but she didn't have anything in her own wardrobe that would work for a club. Worried about exposing the cicatrices on her back, she tugged the top of the dress up, but then, showing too much leg, she pulled at the hem. "I think we look very purple."

Suzanna beamed. "Come on! Let's go have fun!"

Suzanna was right, she passed fifty kwacha into the bouncer's mitt and he shifted his bulk out of the doorway without a word. It took a few seconds for Grace's eyes to adjust to the dark, smoky club. There were about thirty men, most standing along the bar drinking and bobbing their heads to the music. A few couples sat at booths on the near side of the room. For the most part, the men seemed oblivious to Grace and Suzanna. Grace saw only one man react; he shook his companion sleeping in his lap and pointed at them. The man lifted his head, stared hard and said something to make the other laugh before putting his head down again, this time on the table. The only other woman Grace could see was a lone dancer on the small dance-floor, appearing and disappearing like a specter under the strobe light.

A waiter appeared out of the smoke. "A Fanta, please," Grace shouted above the noise.

"She means two vodka-tonics," Suzanna shouted, narrowing her eyes at Grace. Before the waiter could leave, Grace asked him if he knew Godfredah. The waiter jerked a thumb over his shoulder to the dancing woman. Grace beckoned Suzanna to the dance-floor, where Godfredah was gyrating to a hit by Ma Brrr and the Big Dudes. Up close, Grace could see that Godfredah had a delicate, feminine face under a big curly wig, but had no hips in the short skirt and no breasts in the halter top.

They hovered watching Godfredah until their drinks arrived. Suzanna finished hers in three quick gulps. "Ugh! Tastes like pee!" she shouted but swapped glasses with Grace and drained that drink too. "I thought a gay bar would be fun like the ones in London, but this place is a real dump."

Grace ignored her, grabbed her hand and pulled her onto the dance-floor, where she swung Suzanna to the music until she joined Grace dancing.

"I hate this song," Suzanna complained. Grace maneuvered her into a triangle with Godfredah until she was close enough to be heard.

"Can we go somewhere to talk?" Grace shouted to Godfredah above the music.

Godfredah shook his curls. "Paying customers only," he said, smoothing his wig with both hands.

"I'm a paying customer," Grace shouted back. If God-fredah was surprised at being propositioned by a female, he didn't show it.

"Basic is fifty kwacha."

Grace nodded, wondering what she was agreeing to. Godfredah signaled at the waiter, who shrugged. "Follow me, sweetheart," Godfredah said in her ear and then made for a back exit. Grace tried to follow but Suzanna grabbed her and held on firmly.

"Hey, where are you going?"

She extricated herself from Suzanna's grip. "I need to talk to Godfredah privately about the case. Just order an-other drink and wait for me. I'll be right back."

"This place is a shithole and the drinks taste like piss," Suzanna complained again before heading for the bar. Grace held up her hand with all her fingers spread out and mouthed "Five minutes" before she raced after Godfredah, who had already disappeared through a back door.

"My fifty kwacha, sweetheart."

Grace reached into her bra and gave Godfredah the money. The young man counted out the two twenties and a ten, and tucked them into his own bra before unlocking a door that opened into a space not much bigger than the narrow bed in there.

"Lights on or off?"

"On!"

Godfredah clicked on a bare bulb hanging down from the ceiling, and then closed the door behind them. In the bright light Grace could see that Godfredah wore heavy make-up—his mouth was a slash of red lipstick, rouge covered a constellation of pimples across both cheeks and his eyelids looked heavy in deep, iridescent blue eyeshadow.

Grace didn't know how to start the interview. She wished she could be more like Suzanna who had no problems talking to anyone. She wiped her sweaty hands on the back of her dress and stayed at the door while Godfredah lay down on his stomach on the leopard-print counterpane, reached under the mattress and pulled out a string of condoms in foil packaging. His short silver skirt rode up his thighs, partially exposing red lace underwear. Grace couldn't help but stare at his skinny thighs and narrow buttocks through the lace. She hadn't seen male nudity since the village, spying on the boys swimming in the Nyakawise river, a lifetime ago.

"You like what you see, sweetheart?"

Grace hadn't realized that Godfredah was now looking over his shoulder back at her. She felt embarrassed at being caught, and averted her eyes. There was nothing to look at on the grey, dingy walls. Godfredah giggled. "Don't worry, looking is included in your fifty kwacha." He swung his legs over the edge of the bed and sat with his thighs wide open. Godfredah's immodesty unsettled Grace. He pulled off one condom and bit off the corner of the wrapper. Grace took the condom to stop him. She knew she would lose her nerve and run if he whipped out his penis. "Without a condom, it's an extra fifty." Godfredah sounded cheerful but his eyes were cold and hard. Grace sat down next to him on the thin mattress. She shifted as close to the edge of the bed as she could and pulled at her skirt so that her skin did not touch the bedcover, and tried not to think about what happened on this bed.

Godfredah put his hand high on Grace's thigh, making her jump and throw his hand off. She immediately grabbed it and put it back on her knee so as not to offend him. "Sorry! Sorry, I wasn't expecting that." He didn't seem offended in the least.

"Just tell me where you prefer to start," he said gently.

"Um, can we talk first?"

"Sure, sweetheart, but a basic is thirty minutes. Most of my clients don't last that long but with a woman, I can't promise." Godfredah reached down and tucked a toe that had popped out of his strappy stiletto back in place. His toenails were long and carefully painted in a red that matched his lipstick.

"Do you know Bessy?"

Godfredah sat back up. "No."

"Loveness said you two were friends."

"I don't know any Loveness and I don't know him." Godfredah stood but Grace jumped up and blocked the door. She held him back by the shoulders. Not roughly but firmly.

"Then how do you know Bessy's a boy."

He looked unsure. "Get your hands off me or I'll scream for the bouncer."

Grace lifted her hands and held them up in the air. "My

name is Grace Zulu and I'm Bessy's lawyer. I'm not going to hurt you, I just have a few questions, okay?"

"I don't know anything."

"Please! Bessy really needs your help." Grace sat down and hoped that Godfredah wouldn't bolt. He sighed and sat back down again, but this time he crossed his arms and legs.

"I'm keeping the money."

"Yes, of course!" Grace almost laughed in relief. "How long have you known Bessy?"

"A long time. I was a year ahead of him at school. We were…" Godfredah struggled to find the right words.

"Special friends?" Grace tried to be tactful.

"More like we were both different from everyone else so we hung out. Anyways, I didn't see him much after I dropped out of school but then he showed up here a few months ago and asked me to help him get a job. Said he needed money."

"What kind of job?"

"What kind of job?" Godfredah repeated and started to chuckle. It came as a series of coughs, like an old smoker. Grace's case was going from bad to worse. If male prostitution came out in court, she wouldn't be able to explain that away. She pictured Willbess's battered face and felt furious.

"A friend asks for help and you get him into prostitution!"

"He got himself into it," Godfredah hurled back. "Bessy was in it before me. He had a sugar daddy when we were still in school, telling everyone that his boyfriend's taking him to America to get married. That boy's such a dreamer."

Godfredah sighed and shook his head. "I don't know what happened to his sugar daddy but when he came here, he was working the streets. The streets!" Godfredah traced circles around the leopard spots on the bedspread with a long red nail and shook his head. "You have no idea, Miss Grace."

On the late bus home, Grace occasionally spotted women hiding behind the flame trees on Addis Ababa Drive where they were known to sell themselves, but Godfredah was right, she had no idea.

"Here we're safe, the clients are rich and what other job lets you drink and dance at work?" He rearranged his face into a smile but he had the same cold look he had had earlier when he'd offered her sex without a condom. Grace wondered what could have driven Willbess to prostitution. He came from a good, loving home, why would he do such a thing? To help him, she had to focus and get as many facts as she could about the night in question.

"Were you here the night of the fight?"

Godfredah nodded.

"What happened?"

"When a group of guys came in, Bessy left the dance-floor immediately to talk to one of them. I noticed because we're only supposed to leave the dance-floor with a customer after signaling the barman, who keep tabs and makes sure we pay Mr. MacGyver his twenty kwacha per customer at the end of the night. Bessy looked very angry, which was also strange because he's the kind of person who's always smiling and laughing. They went outside for a minute and then Bessy was right back on the dance-floor."

Godfredah picked up the condom again and rustled the foil wrapper as he spoke.

"What happened outside?"

"How should I know? Maybe he wanted mbasela. People ask us for freebies all the time, but we tell them, no money, no honey, just like you lawyers." Godfredah laughed his cough-y laugh. "Anyways, this mujegga followed Bessy back and punched him. Hit him so hard he fell and just lay there on the floor holding his stomach for a long time. Big Daddy, that bouncer out there, grabbed the man to throw him out, but his friends jumped him from behind. These guys tried some kung fu on Big Daddy and the place went crazy. He really beat the shit out of all of them. Someone should've warned them that you don't fuck with Big Daddy."

"Did you know any of the men?"

"No. Big Daddy was asking everyone. He said that they needed to pay Mr. MacGyver for the damage to the bar."

"Where can I find Mr. MacGyver?"

Godfredah shrugged. "Never met him."

"Is MacGyver his real name?"

"Noooo, no one uses real names around here. Except Bessy, of course."

"Of course?"

"His full name is Willbess, Bessy for short. And he's Bessy all the time, at home, at school, no matter what people say about him. He's very charming, so he gets away with it most of the time. Not all the time, obviously."

"Did you see Bessy again that night?"

"He disappeared while those guys were fighting Big Daddy. I heard he got arrested the next day but ni wo boza! Bessy would never fight. If he couldn't talk his way out of a fight, he'd just curl up and take the beating."

"He wasn't arrested for fighting."

Godfredah looked confused. "Then what for?"

"He was arrested for having sex with another man."

Godfredah's expression changed to fear and he slid off the bed, squatted down and pulled a duffel bag out from underneath it.

"Could someone have witnessed Bessy having sex with another man that night?" Grace persisted.

Godfredah yanked off his stilettos, shoved them into the bag and pulled out a pair of lace-less blue sneakers. He stomped his feet into them, slung the bag over his right shoulder and made for the door. "I don't want any trouble," he said as he pushed past Grace and rushed out. Grace didn't stop him this time. She watched his silver skirt flashing like a fish in the moonlight until he disappeared, swallowed whole by the night.

When Grace got back into the club, Suzanna had a bottle of vodka and was holding court at the end of the bar, with a semi-circle of men gathered around her. She refilled some of the glasses and then guzzled the rest directly from the bottle. "Another bottle on me!" she shouted to the waiter, but Grace canceled the order and pulled her out of the club.

"Get off me, stupid bitch!"

Grace ignored her. Suzanna always became belligerent when drunk.

"You can't drink like this and drive," Grace reprimanded.

"You drive then." Suzanna tried to thrust the car key at Grace, who parried it.

"You know I don't know how." Grace was good at driving an ox-cart—she would water the oxen, rub the space between their horns and necks before yoking them, and then whisper in their floppy ears. But a car couldn't be coaxed. Grace wished she had paid more attention to how the gears and pedals worked, not that she was planning to learn on this posh Mercedes.

"Learn to drive, dimwit!" Suzanna slurred. "Who doesn't know how to drive? It's simple, simple, simpleton." She poked Grace in the chest with the key. "Idiot-savant. That's what *you* are, with emphasis on the idiot!"

Grace opened all the car windows and kept one hand on the wheel while Suzanna drove back to campus, mainly in one gear. They made it back to the dorm, where Grace undressed her friend and guided her into bed. Suzanna fell asleep immediately with her thumb in her mouth. Grace smiled; she had forgotten that her friend still sucked her thumb in secret. She wiggled out of the boob-tube dress and slipped on one of Suzanna's t-shirts. There was an empty bedframe where a short-lived roommate had slept, but it had no mattress so Grace climbed into the narrow bed with her back against Suzanna's to try to fall asleep.

Worrying about Willbess kept her awake. If the prosecution found out that he worked as a male prostitute, it would be so prejudicial that she was sure to lose her case. Grace had to find out what the Director of Public Prosecutions knew, and maybe she could propose a plea bargain. Suzanna turned and draped her arm around Grace. Now, living apart, Grace missed her touch. Other than handshakes and an occasional pat on the back, nobody touched her. She gently moved Suzanna's arm and tucked it under hers.

When Grace first moved into their dorm room, it had taken her several months to get used to Suzanna grabbing her hand, hanging on her shoulder and hugging her all the time. She seemed to have no concept of personal space; once when Grace came back from the shower in a chitenge, Suzanna pulled the material down in the back and began to count her ndembo, oblivious to Grace's extreme discomfort. It felt too intimate but she couldn't explain why and had to resist the urge to writhe away. Grace tried to lift up her chitenge but Suzanna snatched it back down again. "Don't be embarrassed, they're beautiful, like some sort of black leopard. Come see in the mirror." Grace stared at her at the mention of a leopard, but Suzanna seemed unaware of any special meaning and held open the door of the cupboard where a small square mirror had been screwed into the wood. Grace crouched low and arched her back so she could see. The cicatrices gleamed slightly against her dark skin. She had felt raised edges of skin on her back but had never thought to look at them. Suzanna started counting again and, when done, announced, "Do you know that you have forty spots on your back? Plus the ones on your cheeks, makes forty-four. You told me these ward off evil spirits, so I guess you're protected as fuck!"

Her atate had told her that a nganga, an albino known

to be the most powerful in the country, had appeared the night she was born to put medicine deep into her face and back to protect her from the evil spirits that had snatched her siblings. But whenever her anyina saw Grace's back, she would scream and denounce her atate as demented for allowing this mwabi charlatan to scar their daughter in this unholy way. Her father would absorb the blows until her strength and anger burned itself out. Over the years, as they fought, Grace heard bits and pieces of the story. That all her siblings had died as infants without as much as a fever, proving to her father that they had been bewitched; that he went as far as Mwanjabantu's village to find this famous nganga and had given him all their money; that Grace came out in an amniotic sac causing the midwife to flee in terror; that the nganga violated every taboo and entered the birthing hut to cut away the sac and the umbilical cord; that her mother couldn't see beyond her own shame to accept that the nganga saved Grace's life.

7

"Director of Public Prosecutions" read a small sign embossed in silver lettering. Grace walked in. She was struck by the difference between the DPP's office and DB & Associates. Other than the occasional outburst from Avaristo screaming at someone, DB & Associates was always hushed and a sharp contrast to this bustling hall of activity. About forty desks were crammed in too close to each other, with a mix of lawyers, secretaries and office orderlies marching between and around them like ants. A series of offices with closed doors lined the right side of the room, and on the left side was a row of dirty windows that filtered out almost all of the sunlight. Above, the lights were on but half of the fluorescent tubes had burned out and metal fans whirred hot, stale air in futile circles. The smell of body odor mixed with cologne made Grace queasy.

She looked around for Bwalya, her classmate from law

school, but couldn't find him. A lawyer in a white wig and black gown swooped past her like a fish eagle, dark wings flapping, then perching and settling at a desk close by. As the woman unpinned her wig, Grace asked her where she could find Bwalya Mumba. With a hairpin that she pulled out of her mouth, she directed Grace to the back of the hall.

Grace found Bwalya head down, reading a book in his lap. "Remember me?" Grace began uncertainly. After four years of classes together, she knew him, but they weren't friends.

"Grace! What are you doing here?" he exclaimed, simultaneously closing the book and slipping it into the desk drawer before Grace could see what he was reading. It didn't look like a law book to her.

"I came to see you."

"Really?" Bwalya's eyes shone and crinkled in the corners. He gave her a wide smile revealing deep dimples. In school he'd had dreadlocks and a scraggly beard that covered his face and hid his dimples. His face was surprisingly round and chubby for such a lanky frame; a row of small, even teeth added to his boyish look; and he looked neat and handsome in his suit. Grace could tell that it was a fine fabric.

"I came about a case."

"I see." He looked disappointed. "Let's talk outside. It's a zoo in here. Smells like one too," he added with the small high-pitched laugh that had so grated her nerves in class. She followed him to a back door. At the threshold, he waited to let Grace through first. He gently guided her to the right, and she felt a tingly sensation where his fingers touched her back. Bwalya led her towards a few mismatched tables and chairs under a flamboyant tree that scattered the afternoon sunlight and red flowers across the outdoor café. They both ducked slightly beneath a branch and walked over the carpet of flowers to a table away from the only other two patrons. Bwalya pulled out a chair for Grace, took off his jacket and set it on the back of the other chair, and loosened his tie before he sat down. She noticed blooms of sweat under his arms and decided to keep her jacket on. Their knees accidentally knocked under the small table so he shifted his seat back and stretched his legs out next to her. The soles of his Oxford shoes were covered in dust and crushed flowers.

Bwalya called out to a woman fanning herself inside a kiosk painted red with "Inviting Biting Café" in scrolling white font, like a Coca-Cola advertisement. "Mulishani, Bana Nsansa?" he greeted the woman politely and asked after her daughter. "Please can I have one Coke and a Fanta for my friend." Bwalya turned to Grace. "Is it still Fanta?"

Grace nodded. "How did you know?"

"The Mingling Bar on campus. I remember you with your nose in a book drinking Fanta, scowling at anyone who approached you."

Grace laughed a bit too loudly. She could rarely afford to drink Fanta but the few times she did buy one, she would nurse and savor it as long as possible. She was flattered that he remembered. "It was always the same thing. People only talked to me when they needed help with their work.

Help me study for exams, help me do my assignment—it was annoying."

"I know, I had the same problem," Bwalya said chuckling. He was the class clown and did just enough to scrape through exams every year. His frivolity had irked her at the time; she felt that he had only gotten into law school because of his father's money, and resented that he had taken a slot from someone who, like her, would have worked like a donkey. But today, sweltering under the flamboyant tree, it didn't seem to matter anymore. She rather enjoyed his easy way of being.

Bana Nsansa brought the drinks. She was a box of a woman, as tall as she was wide, as though she had somehow assumed her kiosk's square shape. She wore a shapeless t-shirt and a chitenge, with the President's face printed in duplicate around her wide hips and buttocks. Her breasts and ample arms jiggled as she opened the bottles and set them down in the middle of the table. Bwalya pulled out some crumpled notes from his pocket, flattened them and gave Bana Nsansa a ten kwacha note before stuffing the rest back into his pocket. "Natotela. Please keep the change." He thanked her.

Grace wondered if he was always so generous, or if he was trying to impress her. The woman cupped her hands and clapped a few times, a gesture of gratitude that Grace hadn't seen since she left the village. Bana Nsansa's gestures and clothes marked her as a villager, just as Grace's accent and ndembo had marked her. She had by now mostly lost her accent, and she carefully covered each cicatrix on her face every morning with make-up. She appreciated that Bwalya was polite to Bana Nsansa. The Londoners were rude to people they called "the help." They were rude to her too and called her "the villager," supposedly in jest.

Bwalya picked up his Coke and tapped its narrow neck against the Fanta bottle. "Chileshe!" The bottles had beads of sweat and bits of ice still clinging to them. The Fanta felt cold under Grace's fingers and tasted so good she downed it all in noisy gulps. "I guess you were thirsty." Bwalya laughed. She didn't mind him teasing her. Who knew that such a cute face had been hidden under those hideous dreads and scruffy beard? A slight breeze rustled the leaves and shook the flowers off their stems but brought no relief from the heat. Bwalya looked up to the sky. "It's hot as hell. I wish the rains would come." She followed his gaze upwards through the branches and could see that the sky was as pale blue and delicate as a starling egg.

"It will rain in the next few days," Grace stated matter-of-factly.

"You sound like my grandmother. Do you have an arthritic knee too?"

"No, I grew up on a farm." Grace knew it was an exaggeration to attach the label "farm" to the small maize fields where she and her mother fought losing battles against the elements, praying for rains to end the drought and then for the floods to stop. You learn to pay close attention to the environment when planting at the right time means the difference between eating and starving. "You can tell the rains are coming by the color of the sky and the scent in the air."

"Wow, you're a triple threat, smart, beautiful *and* you can predict the weather."

Grace blushed. At university, she regarded boys as the unwelcome pests following Suzanna around. Suzanna had advised her to try to be less intimidating, whatever that meant, but Grace was glad that the boys didn't bother her. She didn't have the luxury of failing like Suzanna; she had to be focused on her studies and do well to keep her scholarship. But now that she had her degree…she started to feel giddy in Bwalya's presence. She resisted the urge to touch his hand and reminded herself that she was there for business.

"So, about the case."

"Mmm." Bwalya took a dainty sip of his Coke.

"The People versus Willbess Mulenga."

"Doesn't ring a bell."

"A juvenile accused of carnal knowledge against the order of nature."

"Bestiality?"

"Homosexuality."

"Oh, *that* case. The DPP is handling that one himself. Who's handling the case on your end?"

"Me."

"You?" Bwalya's eyes bulged.

"I'm just handling the preliminary work. DB, the senior partner, will take over soon." She hoped it would be soon. She had heard from her office mate Mabvuto that DB had extended his sick leave yet again. "I'm trying to find out how strong the evidence is, if the DPP has any witnesses, for example."

"Even if I did know, I couldn't tell you."

"It's not illegal and besides you'd have to reveal it during discovery. A pre-emptive discovery process could help get my client out of jail quickly with a plea bargain."

"There's no such thing as pre-emptive discovery."

"Come on, a plea bargain gets Willbess out of jail *and* gets the DPP his conviction. It's a win-win."

Bwalya shook his head slowly. "No chance; the DPP doesn't want a win-win, he wants a win, full stop, exclamation point. He's been ranting about divine law, and how he won't allow Lusaka to become Sodom or Gomorrah."

"I thought lawyers are supposed to uphold common law, not divine law."

"From what I know, common law and divine law agree on this one."

"It's been three weeks since I got this case, and eight since that poor boy was locked up, and absolutely nothing has moved. I don't even know what to tell the family anymore. I can't even get a date for a bail hearing. How is this the law?"

"Hey, hey, don't bite *my* head off." Bwalya raised his palms. "I'm just telling you that the DPP has strong feelings about this case so don't waste your time trying to plea bargain."

Grace put her head in her hands and pressed her eyes with her thumbs, trying to banish the image of Willbess's swollen face. What good is a lawyer who can't do a damn thing for her client? She rose quickly, scraping thick lines in the sand with her chair. "Sorry to have bothered you."

"Come on, Grace, don't leave all pissed off."

Grace used a pen to scratch under her braids while staring at the eucalyptus tree outside DB & Associates. The wind blew a lemony fragrance into her office. The warm breeze was no relief from the November sun, or the cicadas that screeched for rain at top decibel, but Grace kept the window open. She inhaled deeply, the smell of eucalyptus reminding her of university. When she had first arrived from the village, she thought that she was in heaven—green lawns, a lake full of tiny fish and tall eucalyptus that made the campus smell sweet. She'd roamed around marveling at the buildings— the lecture halls, cafeterias, dorms, the chapel with stained-glass windows and her favorite place, the library. Five floors full of books on law, literature, mathematics and philosophy, which she learned meant the love of wisdom. She felt like a philosopher, studying her law books and browsing the shelves on other floors, selecting an eclectic range of books that piqued her interest. She could study uninterrupted in the library without scavenging for time between hoeing, watering, weeding, picking, pulling, gathering, pounding, cooking. She could study without worrying about army worms, stalk borers, leafhoppers or the elements that seemed to conspire against the village, alternating between floods and drought, and yet another crop failure, yet another famine. At university, water gushed out of taps with a twist of her wrist, a full meal landed on her tray in the cafeteria and one flick of a switch and she had lights to study all night.

Grace had loved law school. In the cases she studied, lawyers presented clever arguments, the courts were fair, the judges wise and their decisions just. There was nothing in her law books about battered clients, corrupt cops, a system that would abuse procedure to deny a person justice, or a surly court clerk who told her yet again to check back the next day for a bail-hearing date. Bwalya was a dead-end, and Avaristo was on her back about her low billable hours. She had to work through a large stack of conveyancing to appease Avaristo, but her mind was on Willbess. At least she had caught up with her other work, and was back to Bessy's case.

"Having a nice little reverie on company time?" Grace hadn't heard Avaristo walk into her office.

"Afternoon, Mr. Daka." She rushed back to her desk.

"Christ, those buggers make such a racket." He closed the windows against the cicadas, and then pointed at the empty desk across from Grace. "Where's that ne'er-do-well Mabvuto?" Grace shrugged; she hadn't seen him all day but that wasn't unusual, Mabvuto was often out playing golf. "I swear I would have fired him long ago if he wasn't my nephew. I should state for the record that he's not a blood relative. He's my nephew-in-law. The wife insists that I keep him here, but God knows my five-year-old has more intelligence in her pinkie finger. The only thing he's good for is golf."

"He brings in lots of clients from the golf club. He says he's the firm's rainmaker."

"That moron? Oh please!" Avaristo pointed at a neat pile of files in Grace's out-tray. "My Merit Bank conveyances?"

Grace nodded. "I double-checked them. The bank documents and tax forms are all in order."

"I'll be the judge of that. What's that you're working on?" Avaristo pulled the open folder on Grace's desk towards him and sat down. He checked the name of the case typed neatly on the front of the file. "Hmm, the Mulenga case." He gave a little frown. "And where are you with the research?"

Grace hesitated. She didn't want to get into the details of her night at the MacGyver, but she also didn't want Avaristo to think that she hadn't done her homework. "His sister and a friend confirmed that Willbess is gay. Not that it proves or disproves the charges, but it could be used against him."

"Of course."

"Only the night of the alleged crime should matter to the court."

"In theory," Avaristo said as he leafed through the folder, stopping at the copy of the bail application. "When's the bail hearing?"

"I'm still waiting for a court date."

Avaristo shook his head. "Maybe I can talk to the DPP, offer time-served plus community service with a church to atone to God and country. Then we can go back to billable work and live happily ever after."

"My friend at the DPP's office says he won't consider a plea bargain."

Deep furrows appeared across Avaristo's forehead. "Who told you to talk to the DPP's office?"

"I only talked to a friend who works there."

Avaristo put his elbows on the table and massaged his temples as he muttered under his breath. He then looked up and stared at Grace with his fish eyes. "I told you to do research and file the bail application. Did I give you permission to speak to the DPP's office?"

"My friend said the DPP's on a religious crusade and won't consider a plea."

"You're a first-year associate with *zero* authority to speak for the firm."

"It wasn't anything official."

Avaristo slammed the folder on her desk and made Grace jump in her seat. "Only partners can speak to outside agencies. Are you a partner?" Grace shook her head slowly, unsure whether he expected her to answer. "We can't have moron associates running around making deals. You are *never* to speak for the firm again, you understand?" He picked up the Merit Bank folders and stalked out.

She was surprised when Avaristo returned a half-hour later all smiles, a pile of folders under each arm. "Good work on the Merit Bank conveyances. Flawless." In a scooping motion Avaristo maneuvered the folders into two untidy stacks on Grace's desk. "More conveyances for you." He tapped one pile of folders. "Law is a pie-eating contest, where the prize is more pie."

"I like pie," Grace replied sincerely, to which Avaristo roared with laughter. Grace smiled back uncertainly. She didn't understand what was so funny but felt relieved that he wasn't still angry with her.

Avaristo finally stopped laughing and wiped his eyes with a purple handkerchief that matched his tie. "Ahh, I needed that. It's been a long time since I laughed so hard that I cried. Grace, about earlier…um, let's just say I'm under a lot of pressure. Not an excuse, but an explanation. Can you manage the Mulenga case *and* help me with the Merit Bank bailout?" Grace nodded, beaming. After Avaristo left her office, she opened the window again and half sat on the desk watching the sun sink as she listened to the cicadas last song. It was going to be another long night, but she was happy.

8

Grace found Mrs. Njavwa reading in her favorite black leather armchair with rips on the armrests. The rest of her furniture was black corduroy, faded to grey in some spots and completely bald in others. Her living room was lined wall to wall with shelves crammed with a lifetime's collection of romance novels. Mrs. Njavwa pulled down her glasses so that they hung on their chain around her neck, and put down her book.

"You're home early. Good, we'll have dinner together for a change."

David, Mrs. Njavwa's small white dog, wandered in behind Grace and sniffed at her feet. He was completely blind but seemed to get around just fine. Grace bent over and petted him while he licked her dusty shoes.

"Don't do that, Davey." Mrs. Njavwa scooped up the dog, placed him on his back in the crook of her arm and rocked and nuzzled him like a baby. "It's your favorite to-night, goat stew."

Grace wasn't sure if her landlady was talking to her or to the dog. She went to her room to wash up and when she came back, food was on the table. Mrs. Njavwa was sitting with Davey on her lap feeding him small pieces of goat meat. It still irked Grace that Mrs. Njavwa's dogs ate better than most people, but she wasn't going to bring it up again. Mrs. Njavwa had already told her that what she fed her small poodle-mix, David, and her giant Rhode-sian Ridgeback, Goliath, wasn't Grace's business and if she didn't like it, she could leave. Mrs. Njavwa was like that, the sweetest old lady until you said anything against those she loved, especially her dogs.

"Grace, you're not eating. What's wrong?" Mrs. Njavwa asked, her rheumy eyes going back and forth between Grace's full plate and her own empty one. "You usually wolf down your food faster than Goliath."

"Problems with a case of mine," Grace replied.

"Which case?" Mrs. Njavwa perked up. Grace got the feel-ing that her landlady tried to live vicariously through her. The nights Grace made it home for dinner, Mrs. Njavwa pumped her for information about her day. She loved to hear stories about Grace's colleagues, especially Avaristo. She wanted de-tails on the most mundane of legal tasks and asked endless questions. She wouldn't let Grace get away with pleading confidentiality. "You don't need to name names. Go on, tell me," she would insist, pushing more food on Grace, who was normally happy to keep eating.

"Is it that nasty Avaristo?"

Grace laughed. "No. This time I think it's nasty Grace."

"Tell me."

Grace told her everything. Mrs. Njavwa sat with her head cocked so that her good ear was towards Grace, and closed her eyes, as if that helped her hearing. Words spilled out of Grace. She spoke for a long time and Mrs. Njavwa listened without interrupting her. It felt good to talk, as though a calabash full of water had been lifted off her head. She told her about Bessy, how his family hadn't been allowed to see him, how he had been beaten up, and how Grace herself had been shoved to the ground by the policeman. "Officer Lungu didn't care that I'm a lawyer. All he saw was a gay boy and a village girl he could abuse with impunity." She talked about Mrs. Mulenga and how she had vented her frustration on Grace, and how Bessy was stuck in prison, and how it felt impossible to fight the system. "They grind you down until you want to give up before you even get into court." She told Mrs. Njavwa how her so-called friend at the DPP's office refused to lift a finger, and the court clerk was downright obstructionist. "I got into a shouting match with that kaponya at the court. With him it's always, 'Come back tomorrow,' like it isn't his job to set the hearing date. It's almost the end of the year now and it's still the same story." On her last trip to the clerk of court's office, a small windowless room near the side entrance of the court, her frustration boiled over. She remembered the words "utterly incompetent," "waste of space" and "moron" tumbling out of her mouth. Grace

THE LIONS' DEN   105

had somehow internalized Avaristo's language and now she worried that Bessy would pay the price.

Mrs. Njavwa opened her eyes. "And how is fighting with everyone working for you?"

"What?" Grace had expected sympathy from Mrs. Njavwa, but there was none in her eyes. "I don't want to fight, Mrs. Njavwa, I have to! I'm fighting for Bessy."

Mrs. Njavwa sighed and then unwound her headscarf, showing Grace a bald patch on her head. She ran her fingers up and down a long scar. This was the first time Grace had seen Mrs. Njavwa without a head-covering. She looked even older with her small head of cropped grey hair and a bald shiny circle around an ugly scar.

"Did you know I was a freedom fighter in the independence struggle?"

Grace nodded. Apropos or not, Mrs. Njavwa started almost every story about her youth with, "Did you know I was a freedom fighter?"

"It was just before independence, and me and the gang, as we called ourselves, met in Father Sebastian's office. KK was going to announce his first cabinet and you can't imagine how excited we were. Independence was set for October 24, 1964, and all our dreams were about to come true. We waited and waited until KK finally arrived. I remember he was wearing a new Chairman Mao suit and he looked so handsome and presidential. He acted like it too, not even greeting us properly, just waving his white handkerchief at us." Mrs. Njavwa imitated a royal wave. "Then he started announcing his cabinet. First it was Reuben for vice president, then Mainza, and Sikota, and so on and so forth, and we all cheered and clapped until he finished making his appointments. Everyone in the gang had a cabinet post except me. Even a white man, Mr. Skinner, who wasn't part of the gang, was appointed the Minister of Justice, but not me and not a single woman. When we realized that all the positions were filled and I had been left out, there was a stunned silence. It was so quiet you could hear a pin drop, at least until I lost it. After all I'd done for the struggle and everything I sacrificed, I had nothing but this big gash in my head. You can't imagine how furious I was that day and I really let him have it, right there and then in front of everyone."

"That must have been something to see."

"Oh yes! Father Sebastian said I was like a spitting cobra," Mrs. Njavwa hissed at Grace. "But do you know what happened next?"

Grace shook her head.

"From that day onward I was out in the cold. And it wasn't just KK, it was all of them. They wouldn't meet me, or take my calls. We had been so close and made many plans together so things would be better for the next generation, for you girls. I felt betrayed by all of them."

Grace thought of her mother and felt a sharp pang in her chest. No matter what Father Sebastian preached, betrayal was unforgivable and Grace could *never* forgive her mother.

Mrs. Njavwa continued, "In hindsight, I realized that KK was right. All I knew was fighting. Fight! Fight! Fight!" Mrs. Njavwa lifted a fist into the air. "I was a freedom fighter and it was a good thing during the struggle, but independence was a time for diplomacy, and I didn't know how to play nice. I was a hothead like you, but if you don't learn when to fight and when to use diplomacy, you'll fail too. Do you understand?"

Grace was surprised. She thought of herself as reserved and measured and got angry only when the situation warranted it. She felt defensive. "Righteous anger is not the same as being a hothead. Calling KK out was the right thing to do."

Mrs. Njavwa sighed and put her doek back on, wrapping and tucking the long scarf back into a neat turban. "Being right won't buy you a bunch of bananas. If I could go back in time, Grace, I would've done things differently. All I did that day was prove KK right, that I wasn't cabinet minister material. He had the pressure of a whole new country on his shoulders, the last thing he needed was me screaming like a hyena as if it was my right to be in his cabinet. It was sixty-four and no one was appointing women in those days, but had I given him time, stayed in his inner circle, I'm sure that I could have shown him that I was the right man for the job. The right person, I mean."

"You don't know that."

Mrs. Njavwa sighed. "Well, I know what didn't work. Fighting friend and foe alike allows your enemies to gain ground. If you want my advice, Grace, go and make amends. Start with that good-for-nothing at the court, take him a Fanta and a fritter and apologize."

"Amends? My client has been stuck in jail for months

instead of being out on bail because of him. I'm not apologizing to that kaponya."

"Well, what about the boy from university? Sounds to me like he was just doing his job. Take him out for a nice meal and let him talk. Men love to talk. Stroke his ego a bit, you never know what he'll share."

Grace shook her head. She had no intention of spending her hard-earned money on Bwalya.

"I'm empowering you with wisdom, my child, what you do with it is up to you. Now eat your food, or I'll give it to Davey."

At the sound of his name, David materialized from under the table. He stared in Mrs. Njavwa's direction as she left the table, but didn't follow her to bed as he usually did. When she was gone he shifted his blue, cloudy eyes in Grace's direction.

"What are you staring at? How do you still see everything, little one?" She marveled at how this blind little dog dashed around the house and garden at full speed, and played, nipped and bit Goliath without getting squashed. Grace took a piece of goat meat, shredded it and then bent down to give pieces to the dog. David sat at Grace's feet patiently as she alternated between feeding him and herself. She had missed dinner the last few nights, and it felt good to eat more than biscuits and bananas. The food was cold but spicy and delicious. She thought about Mr. Patel and Priyanka and smiled. "Davey, do you know that spices cure constipations?" Mr. Patel sent Grace letters with news of the village. Nothing there seemed to change—the cycles of floods and droughts; the rotation of stalk borers, army worms, locusts and other pestilence; the young marriages, births and early deaths. And even though Grace never asked in her letters back to him, Mr. Patel always confirmed that her mother was alive and well. She missed him but otherwise didn't miss the village at all. The last time she had seen Mr. Patel had been at her graduation.

Graduation was the best day of Grace's life. A pavilion had been erected in the giant square between the library, the sports hall and the Mingling Bar. It was decorated in the national colors using small triangular flags and layers of shiny material draped across the front. A podium with a microphone sticking out of it had been placed on the right side, with a dozen chairs behind it and one large, elaborately carved rosewood chair that resembled a throne nearest to it. The graduating students, dressed in their black robes, sat in the first few rows of folding metal chairs, and their families, dressed in their finery, filled the rest of the seats behind them. The early birds got chairs, but many more had to stand at the back. Farther behind in a tight perimeter were policemen in ceremonial black uniforms, with glinting silver buttons.

Grace's last name put her at the end of her row of law students next to a boy from her class, Kenneth Zimba. They had not spoken much in class but this day, buoyed by joy and excitement, they chatted and laughed easily. He pointed to a large, prim-looking family seated near the front and claimed them as his own. Then he told Grace how his parents were in the first cohort of UNZA students in 1966. Kenneth shared that his parents had met, married and had him while at university, "and not in that order!" he added with a hearty laugh. As with many males born after independence, he was named after the President. Kenneth asked where her family was. "Here somewhere." Grace swiveled her neck and began to scan the crowds behind the students. She had sent only two of the five invitations allocated to each graduating student. She was one of the few who had too many of the eggshell-white cards with the university's emblem embossed in copper on top of the elegant serif script inviting esteemed guests to attend the twenty-fourth graduation ceremony. On the back in large black print was a warning that entrance was strictly by invitation. Suzanna said she couldn't make it because the Londoners were arriving the same day, so Grace kept one as a memento, mailed one to Mr. Patel and gave two to a girl from the fifth floor who was going door-to-door begging for extras so that her family of thirteen could all see her graduate. The last one she had mailed to her mother with money for a bus ticket folded into a piece of paper. She had raised the envelope to the sun to be sure that the money was concealed, and hesitated before sticking it into the university's outgoing mail slot in the library. Grace knew it was perverse to test her mother, knowing that she would fail. Her anyina would use the money for something else, of that she was sure. She was so certain that her mother wouldn't come she couldn't fully explain to herself why she had invited her. Maybe it was to prove that she was a good child in spite of her mother's failings, or perhaps it was just spite—the elegant invitation and money a way to force her anyina to feel ashamed for not believing in her daughter. What would she do if her mother showed up? Would they pretend to forgive each other? Grace tried to conjure a scene in her mind with her anyina at graduation, smiling, clapping and waving at her, but she couldn't. She had only seen her mother happy in church. As long as Mr. Patel made it, she told herself, she didn't care.

Grace hadn't seen Mr. Patel yet but she knew that he was there, he wouldn't miss this day. She stood up and searched the crowd until she saw him jumping up and down and waving at her from behind a policeman positioned to keep over-eager parents at bay. She waved back, both arms flapping like a giant ground hornbill trying to take off, and only sat back down when the complaints around her became aggressive.

"You see that man waving frantically behind the policeman?" she said to Kenneth.

"You mean that Indian dude?"

Aside from the jumping and the waving, she had never seen Mr. Patel look so elegant, in a suit and tie with his hair slicked back.

"That's Mr. Patel. He's my only family."

"You're adopted by an Indian family? That's unusual. If he's your dad, why do you call him Mr. Patel?"

She had never thought about it. He had always been Mr. Patel. Her father had called him *Misterpatel*, one word, often said with a sly smile like it was an old joke that was always funny. It didn't matter; the name seemed to work well for someone who was both her atate and her anyina.

Drumbeats and whistles filled the air and everyone fell quiet. A procession of about twenty with drums strapped to their bodies arranged themselves in a straight line in the space between the pavilion and the students. Behind the drummers followed dancers from every part of the country, each tribe trying to outdo the others in style and energy. Grace only recognized the two from Eastern province, where she was from. The Nyau dancers wore red masks, feathers and raffia skirts, and spun and stamped with noisy bells tied to their legs; and the Ngoni warriors were draped in skins of leopards, civets and genet cats and looked fierce waving their sticks and shields. After several dance troupes, Kenneth identified the last as the Lozi royal house from the west. In contrast to the rest, the Lozi were elegant in their red berets, layers of ivory bangles and colorful siziba; they moved in perfect unison, as if rowing their Litunga across the floodplains to higher land. The crowd watched mesmerized until they, followed by the drummers, disappeared behind the library.

When the crowd turned their heads back, President Kaunda was walking across the pavilion in front of them. He looked magnificent in a black velvet cap with a gold rim and tassel; a green gown with an intricate, embroidered design down the front and along the edges of its bell sleeves; and a copper-colored hood. The university chancellor and the lecturers followed at a distance in their own gowns of black, crimson, baby blue and purple. The President went straight to the podium and waved his white handkerchief.

"My fellow countrymen and countrywomen," President Kaunda began, sweeping a beatific smile across the crowd like a lighthouse, "it's with great pride that I as Grand Chancellor of the University of Zambia confer upon our students their diplomas today. Join me in congratulating our graduates."

Grace leapt to her feet along with everyone else and clapped and ululated. The President gazed at the students and waved his handkerchief again until they sat down.

"I congratulate you families, you wonderful lecturers and also I must congratulate myself. The World Bank told me it isn't wise to invest so much of our limited resources in higher education, they said to me, 'Mr. President, your poor country can't afford these subsidies. Even rich countries aren't doing what you are doing. The investment in education is too costly and unsustainable.'"

People in the crowds booed.

"How can they tell me that investing in this university is unsustainable? You all know that I was once a teacher and I will always be a humble teacher in my heart, so no one can tell me not to invest in you. I told them, 'World Bank, what you propose is intolerable and illogical because you'll bring this country to its knees.' They are trying to undermine our future and I could never agree to that so I told them, 'Pack your bags!'"

The crowd was back on their feet again clapping and shouting in agreement.

"Looking into your faces, my dear graduates, I see a brilliant future for our beloved country despite the trouble you give me with your strikes and riots. What do you have to complain about, my ungrateful children? Why are you biting this hand that feeds you?"

Grace held her breath, waiting for him to lambast them and ruin their graduation ceremony, but Kaunda just shook his head and cackled; only then did the crowd laugh along with him.

"I'm the father of this great nation and you are my children, so whether you deserve it or not, I will always invest everything I have in you."

Afterwards, Mr. Patel took photos of Grace by the university's lake, then asked a passing student to take a picture of them together. "Less teeth, Gracie, look serious now!" But she couldn't stop smiling. When the roll was finished, Mr. Patel took it carefully out of the back of the camera, placed it in its small cylindrical container, put it in the inner pocket of his suit, then hung the camera around his neck. They strolled arm-in-arm around the sparkling lake, talking about the ceremony as if it was a fond memory that hadn't just happened. Mr. Patel explained the different tribes and their distinct traditional garb and dances, not that Grace could remember all the details. He reminded her how everyone had clapped and ululated when Grace was awarded top law student and went up to the podium to shake hands with the President. How the President had called her the brightest in a constellation of shining stars.

"On this rare occasion, I agree with the President. Your future is as bright as the sun glittering on this lake. Tell me again about your job as a high-powered lawyer."

"I told you, I'll just be a first-year associate."

"Just? You'll be just like Gandhi, defending the defenseless."

"I have to learn the trade first." Whatever Grace said, Mr. Patel didn't seem to grasp that she was going to be a corporate lawyer, not a public defender.

"Yes, my dear Gracie, even Gandhi had to start somewhere."

"I thought you said you were out of tears," Grace said, noticing his eyes welling up again, and squeezed his arm.

With his free hand, he extracted a crusty handkerchief from his pocket and blew his nose noisily. "Today is a day of utmost happiness with only a small touch of sadness. I so wish your father was here to see his dream come true."

"I feel him. It's been a long time but today I feel Atate again." Grace's ndembo had felt warm all day. There were no msolo trees on campus, but the willow trees surrounding the lake were leafy enough to conceal an ancestor.

9

"I was surprised by your invitation, Grace. A happy surprise, I mean," Bwalya said as they sat down. "Mr. Pete's is one of my favorite restaurants."

More than a month of trying and still no bail-hearing date, Grace was now desperate enough to take Mrs. Njavwa's advice and try diplomacy. She needed something that could help her force a plea bargain, or better still, if she could confirm that the DPP had insufficient evidence, she could push for a *nolle prosequi* and have the charges dropped.

"I've never actually been here before but I've heard good things about the steak," Grace said. Suzanna had called Mr. Pete's a cool dive where the steaks were cheap but good.

"The steaks are amazing but the real secret is the hot sauce. Legend has it that long ago Mr. Pete sold his soul to the devil for the recipe."

Grace looked around the long dark room filled with

high-backed wooden benches and tables, the open kitchen at one end with a giant black barbeque pit that hissed and belched smoke like an old dragon. Bwalya had sat down next to Grace rather than across from her. They faced the kitchen and watched a leathery chef toss Mosi beer over sirloins, tenderloins, fillets and racks of ribs. The chef's thin fingers moved constantly, his eyes trained on the meat, oblivious to the hypnotic effect of his snapping silver tongs, the flying arcs of golden beer and the amber flames blackening the meat. The aroma made Grace dizzy with hunger.

A waiter appeared to take their order. Grace looked at the prices on a chalkboard and realized it was Suzanna cheap, not Grace cheap, and started calculating how many days of wages one dinner would cost her. She already regretted listening to Mrs. Njavwa. She wasn't even sure if Bwalya could or would help her, but he was her only hope. She knew the DPP didn't want to plea bargain, but as far as she could tell, his decision was emotional, not rational. If they lacked evidence, Grace felt confident that she could pressure the DPP to negotiate.

"Mulishani, ba kalimba. Welcome back, boss. The usual?" The waiter shook Bwalya's hand vigorously and flashed a mangled set of teeth at Grace.

"Shani, boi. Yes, the usual for me, and is fillet steak good for you too?" Grace nodded, unsure what the differences were between the many steaks listed on the chalkboard. "A beer for me, and Grace, what would you like to drink?"

"Fanta, please."

"Come on, have a real drink. Mosi? Wine? Whatever you want. And boi, put this on my tab, dinner's on me."

"But I invited you," Grace protested, but not too much.

Bwalya waved his hand in the air. "I appreciate the invite but I insist. Boi, don't take any money from my friend."

Grace felt relieved that she didn't have to worry about the size of bill. "Fanta's fine. I don't drink alcohol."

Bwalya nodded to the waiter and the man disappeared. "You don't drink at all? On campus, you and Boozy Suzy were always glued at the hip, I just assumed—"

"Don't call her that!" Grace cut him off and it came out sharper than she had intended.

Bwalya seemed unfazed. "It's just a nickname, and she did kinda earn it, zonking out all over campus. I remember once I saw you carry *Su-zaa-naa* out of the boys' dorms over your shoulder. I was impressed but also a bit scared of how freakishly strong you are." He grabbed her arm, folded it and squeezed her biceps.

Grace pulled her arm away. "That's not a very polite thing to say," she protested but his high-pitched laughter set her off too.

"It's true! Suzanna is definitely on the plump side, and you hoisted her over your shoulder like she was nothing—" he made a tossing motion over his shoulder "—like a sack of balloons."

"More like a sack of bricks!" she corrected. It seemed funny now but Grace had been livid that night. Suzanna had refused to leave the party and kept drinking until she passed out, but not before telling Grace to fuck off in front of everyone. The few other girls at the party had already drifted off but Grace would never leave Suzanna alone with so many boys. She didn't recall Bwalya being there that night, but did remember carrying Suzanna across campus. She'd been struggling up the stairway of the girls' dorm when Suzanna threw up on her. "You missed the best part, she vomited down my back." Bwalya burst into laughter again, but then Grace began to feel disloyal and stopped laughing. "Suzanna can overdo things sometimes, but she's a good person. She's helped me a lot, especially my first year before I got a scholarship. I don't think I'd have managed without her. University was so different from where I grew up."

"You mentioned that you grew up on a farm. That must've been cool."

"To be honest, I grew up in a village and we had a small plot to grow crops to eat, with a bit left over to sell. We were subsistence farmers." She watched for Bwalya's reaction, worried that he would be turned off by her humble background. His eyebrows knitted together but he shifted closer to her and stretched his arm out behind her like a protective wing.

"I've never been to a village. What's it like?"

In that moment she wanted to share everything with him but she heard Suzanna's voice in her head: No one wants to hear about other people's depressing shit! Grace would focus on the best things about the village. "Nyamphande's in a valley with a river running through it. It's very fertile, with maize fields in every direction as far as the eye can see, and hundreds of mango trees everywhere. They're really sweet and they grow to this size," she said, shaping her hands into a big ball. "In the rainy season, the trees are dripping with fruit." I can't believe that I am talking about stupid mangoes on a date, she thought to herself.

But Bwalya was nodding and smiling. "Ooh, mangoes are my favorite. I would love the village." His little white teeth gleamed.

"Once, I ate fifteen mangoes in one go," she boasted.

Bwalya looked impressed. "Wow! That's crazy."

He would be less impressed if she told him that she had eaten so many because she had had nothing else to eat that day, or that she spent the night in the outhouse in agony. One day she would tell him everything about her life in the village. About the drought that dried up the river and killed their crops, about her father having to leave the land he loved to work twelve-hour shifts in a mine, about the Chief seizing most of their land after her father died so they could barely grow enough to survive, about running away when her mother tried to marry her off to the same Chief. One day, but not today, she thought. All she said to him was, "After my dad died, things got hard but I managed to get to university, get my degree and the rest is history."

Bwalya took her hand in his and squeezed it gently. "Sorry about your father."

Grace attempted a smile. Her father's death was definitely in the category of depressing shit that she would not be talking about with Bwalya that night. Before he could ask any more questions about the village, Grace asked about his family.

"Not much to tell. My parents were both economics professors, so I grew up in academic housing on campus. We moved to a big government house in Woodlands when the President appointed my dad to manage the government's money, and my mum still teaches."

"She teaches at *our* university?"

"Yup, the one and only university in the country. So you can imagine, she takes my bad grades very personally. My young brother's in first year and is proving to be a dullard like me. Thank God for my older sister. She's in her last year of medical school and saving our family name from ruin. The women in my family have all the brains, so thanks to them, I'm comfortable dating a genius like you."

It was presumptuous of Bwalya to state that they were dating, but Grace's insides warmed and she didn't challenge him; instead she said, "I work very hard, that's all. You would've done much better if you weren't so lazy."

"Wow! Now look who's not being polite."

"It's true!"

They chatted and giggled and Bwalya held her hand under the table and didn't let go until the waiter brought out their steaks on sizzling platters, maneuvering them onto the table with great care.

"Natotela, boi."

"Thank you," Grace echoed. She almost drooled at the meat hissing on the metal plates and the baked potatoes quietly oozing butter.

Bwalya inspected an array of bottles in the middle of the table, selected one and handed it to Grace. "This is the infamous hot sauce. The peri-peri spices will rip off the roof of your mouth, so careful. Just a tiny bit."

Grace turned the bottle upside down and tapped the bottom until a gob of thick red paste plopped onto her plate. She stuck her pinkie into the sauce and put it into her mouth and sucked. It had a nice flavor but wasn't hot. She grinned, thinking she would impress him with her chili-eating skills. She picked up the bottle and this time smacked the bottom several times until there was a pool of red goop between her meat and potato. Bwalya watched her intently with his eyebrows raised. She explained, "I grew up eating hot food. My dad's best friend, Mr. Patel, had a store about thirty kilometers from our village. Now *his* food was hot. Much hotter than this stuff." She was about to taste it again but remembered that she shouldn't stick her fingers into her food. Grace picked up her knife and fork and cut off a small piece of steak, dipped it delicately into the sauce and put it in her mouth. The steak was perfect, bloody and charred with fatty bits still clinging to its edges, and the hot sauce left a lingering heat on her tongue. "Mmm." She nodded at Bwalya.

He beamed. "Told you." Bwalya picked up his utensils and started to eat too.

Grace resisted the urge to wolf down her steak. She took another small bite and focused on what Mrs. Njavwa called nice manners, not eating too fast, not talking with her mouth full, not using her fingers, and dabbing the sides of her mouth often with her napkin.

"Mr. Patel is the reason I became a lawyer. He, my dad and Gandhi." She remembered that after lunch at Mr. Patel's she would lie on a reed mat and play with his cat, the previous Priyanka, and pretend not to listen as he and her father got drunk on kachasu, laughed, complained and cried together. She liked it better when they were feeling optimistic and talked about the future, when Mr. Patel would open up a chain of shops, her father would be a commercial tobacco farmer, and Grace would follow in Gandhi's steps and become a famous lawyer.

"Gandhi?"

"Yes, they always said it was my destiny, but I didn't really believe it until Mr. Patel told me about a man called Gandhiji who was born poor like us, but became such a powerful lawyer that he single-handedly ended British rule in India. Of course I know it wasn't as simple as that now, but for some reason, as a girl, the story of Gandhi made it seem possible for me too. So as far back as I can remember, I wanted to be a lawyer."

"And so, because of Gandhi, you became a corporate lawyer?"

"I bet you didn't know that Gandhi started his career as a corporate lawyer too."

"No. Really?"

"Yes. He only became the famous Gandhi we all know much later in his life. Besides, I won't be a corporate lawyer forever, and I get to work on pro bono cases, as you already know." She glanced at Bwalya, who nodded.

"I know the case is important to you, so let me see what I can find out."

"Thanks." Grace tried to act casual but couldn't help smiling. Mrs. Njavwa was right after all. There was a time for diplomacy. She had been so diplomatic that she had the promise of good information for her case *and* her first boyfriend.

"Is your mum still in the village?"

"Yup." Grace's smile vanished at the mention of her mother, but she quickly arranged her face into a neutral expression.

"You must miss her."

Not one bit, she thought as she pretended to be too focused on the last bite of her potato to answer. Bwalya drained the rest of his beer in one long swig. He hadn't touched his food for a while and his knife and fork lay neatly together on the side of his plate.

"Are you going to eat that?" Grace asked. He had left a quarter of his steak and half a potato.

"Nah, too full of beer." Bwalya patted his flat stomach.

"May I?" Grace knew that Mrs. Njavwa would not approve, but this was steak! Bwalya looked amused as he swapped plates with her, handed her the hot sauce and ordered her another Fanta.

10

Grace found Father Sebastian in his office behind St Ignatius's. Unlike the ornate church with vaulted ceilings and
mosaics of stained glass, his office was a simple box with
four white walls, a plain wooden cross nailed to one and a
pinboard of photos on another next to a mukwa desk. On
the desk, lunch was set for one.

"Grrrace! Come in, my child." Despite leaving Germany
more than fifty years ago, Father Sebastian still spoke with
a strong German accent, rolled r's, soft z's and w's for v's.
Grace had gotten to know the priest from Bible study on
campus. While they did discuss the Bible, mainly they sang
modified pop songs while Father Sebastian played his guitar. "I just learned to play a nice song by Milli Wanilli!"
he would say, and teach them the song with his own lyrics:
"*Ooh, ooh, ooh, God loves you.*" He was so unlike the Catholic priests Grace had grown up with, all fire and brim-

stone. As a child, Grace thought brimstone was the English word for drought, because that was her experience of hell.

"I've missed you at church these past Sundays."

"Sorry, Father. I've been working weekends."

"*Ja*, Mrs. Njavwa told me that you're working far too hard." Father Sebastian had not only connected Grace to Mrs. Njavwa, but also negotiated a rate for room and board that she could afford. "Promise me you'll come for Christmas mass. The choir has been putting in extra practice for the service. It will be beautiful. *Sehr schoen.* Surely you'll make time for the birth of Christ?"

"I'll be there, Father."

"Good. And I hope to see more of you in 1991. No one should be too busy for church, you must make time to nourish your soul. Speaking of nourishment, come and eat with me."

Grace hesitated. "I can come back in a bit."

"Nonsense. You will join me. Sit down." He pointed to the chair. "There's plenty more food in the kitchen. I'll go heat this up and find you a plate." Before Grace could protest, he picked up his plate and darted out of the room.

While she waited, Grace examined the photos on the large board next to his desk, each one pinned on with a single thumbtack. Many were faded black-and-white pictures of a thin, young priest. Grace immediately recognized Father Sebastian's fabulously bushy eyebrows. In old age they remained just as thick and inexplicably black, while the hair on his head had turned completely white and had thinned to a few strands. She looked at the collection of photos taken over his decades in Zambia—Father Sebastian holding babies in baptism gowns, beaming between brides and grooms, playing with children. She smiled at one of him dancing with a gaggle of women, a chitenge wrapped over his cassock. When the priest walked back into his office holding a tray, she was looking at a black-and-white photo of him with a young President Kaunda playing guitars together.

Grace pointed to the photo. "Mrs. Njavwa mentioned that you often helped the gang during the independence struggle. Do you know the President well?"

"I *knew* KK during the independence struggle. In fact, he's the one who introduced me to Mrs. Njavwa and her husband. David was still alive back then." He put the tray down on the table. "We held meetings in the church, right under Governor Evelyn Hone's nose." Father Sebastian tapped his large nose and chuckled. "I smuggled KK all around Northern Rhodesia in the back of my Zephyr under a blanket. Sometimes he had to hide in the trunk. But we haven't spoken in a long time now." His eyes changed to the palest blue. It fascinated Grace that his eyes could change color. "KK stopped listening when I started saying things he didn't want to hear. About becoming more repressive. These were the very things we had all fought against."

The priest moved the plates off the tray and then sat down to eat. He dug through the crust of the nshima and immediately pulled his fingers out. "*Scheisse!*" he shrieked in German, shaking his fingers and then sucking them. Steam escaped from the dish. "Eat!" he commanded, pushing the food closer to her, even though it was already within her reach.

Grace carefully took a lump of nshima, rolled it in her hand, thumbed the chicken stew, beans and pumpkin leaves into a ball, and expertly scooped everything into her mouth without dripping. They both ate with their hands, hunching over their food. Between mouthfuls, Father Sebastian pointed with his knuckle to the photo of himself and President Kaunda.

"Kenneth used to be a good guitar player, but he doesn't practice enough. When you're the President it doesn't matter, everyone claps like you're Jimi Hendrix. You know Hendrix?" Grace shook her head. "You'd like his music. I'll make you a cassette tape." One day Grace would be able to afford a cassette player to listen to all the tapes that Father Sebastian had made for her. "Hendrix was one of the greats. May his soul rest in peace."

"He's dead?"

"Yah, he died so young, but I believe he is in heaven rrriffing for our Lord."

"How did he die."

"Alcohol and drugs."

"You believe he still went to heaven?"

"Of course. The Lord forgives all sins. *Though your sins be as scarlet, they shall be as white as snow.*"

Grace nodded. "Isaiah."

"Chapter 1, verse 18. Grace, on the subject, have you thought more about forgiving your mother?"

Grace snorted. Her anger hadn't diminished, in fact with

time its seeds had taken root, grown and sprouted bitter leaves.

"Grace, you must find it in your heart to forgive her. Maybe your mother couldn't see any other way out of a desperate situation."

"Hard to believe that she couldn't find a way that didn't involve selling her only daughter. If it wasn't for Mr. Patel, I'd be married to a man old enough to be my grandfather." Grace shivered at the thought of a life serving the Chief and bearing even more children for him. When she left the village, he already had eleven, most older than her. "And if that's not evil enough, I'll remind you that she also burnt down Mr. Patel's store."

"Forgiving your mother is not saying that she hasn't done terrible things. Think of Jesus, forgiving his murderers as he was being crucified."

"That's why Jesus is Jesus."

Father Sebastian smiled. "He showed us that anything can be forgiven."

Grace looked at her plate of steaming food and remembered how much struggle went into every meal in the village. She remembered pounding maize, picking vegetables, fetching firewood and water, and cooking over a small charcoal brazier for one simple meal of nshima and greens. She also remembered the physical pain of starvation and didn't wish that on anyone, not even her mother. But she wasn't ready to forgive her. "I send her money every month." It stung her to put her hard-earned kwacha into an envelope each time, and she licked each stamp with bitter saliva before mailing it. Although she contemplated it, Grace knew that she could never stop sending her mother money. She could never let her anyina starve.

"That's not the same as forgiveness. Remember, forgiveness is as much for your own sake as your mother's. I'll continue to pray for you." Father Sebastian disappeared and came back with a cloth on his shoulder and a bowl of water, which he put down in front of her. It was warm and the sticky nshima bits easily came off her fingers and stayed floating in the water. He handed her the cloth and while she was wiping her hands, he created a precarious pile on the tray, putting the sloshing water bowl on top of the plates with the clean, white chicken bones and streaks of sauce left after their meal. When Grace was done drying her hands, he used the cloth to cover the mess.

"So what brings you here today, my child?"

"A case of mine."

"A case? I'm a priest, not a lawyer, how can I help?" Father Sebastian leaned back and rested his hands on his bulging stomach, his bushy eyebrows suddenly animated.

"My client was arrested for a homosexual act which, as you probably know, is a crime in Zambia."

"And you're troubled by your client's homosexuality?"

"What? No!" Grace felt insulted that Father Sebastian would think she was like her mother, or the DPP who invoked the Bible in prosecuting Willbess. "What troubles me is the Church. I realize that this is so much bigger than my case and the Catholic Church bears a big part of the responsibility. The Church continues to legitimize this discrimination and even hatred of homosexual people, so I want you to do your part, as I do mine to win this case."

"Grace, I think you are misunderstanding the teaching of the Church. As a boy I was taught to hate homosexuals along with Jewish people, artists, intellectuals and ultimately anyone who didn't support the Fuhrer. I found my salvation in God's love, and I can assure you that I would never support any form of hatred and neither does the Catholic Church. We are not against the sinner, only against the sin."

"And when it's *who* you are? I know I can't change who I am, you can't change who you are either, so why would the Church expect gay people to change?"

"Homosexuality isn't who anyone is, it's a choice."

"Who would choose a life of persecution, of prosecution?" She thought about Mr. Patel. How he was her mother's scapegoat. How she even blamed him for her father's death. After a year or two in Lusaka, Grace realized that her father hadn't died of black lung disease from the mines, as her mother had told her, he had died of AIDS. Grace saw it often enough in Lusaka to look back and recognize it for what it was.

Whoever said it was a gay disease had lied. It was a contagious disease that didn't discriminate between straight, gay, rich, poor, young, old, man, woman, child. They said one in five had it, a modern-day biblical plague, but people still blamed homosexuals. Her mother blamed Mr. Patel, but Grace knew that as close as the relationship was, it was as Mr. Patel had described it, "Best friends, nothing more, nothing less." She suspected that her father had contracted

AIDS on the Copperbelt where he had lived eleven months of the year; AIDS was everywhere in the cities. And even if Mr. Patel and her father's relationship had been romantic, Grace wouldn't have cared. Mr. Patel had been more of a parent to her than her mother ever had been.

"Who'd choose to be a scapegoat for everything that goes wrong in society? It's not a choice, Father. It's just not!"

"The catechism of the Catholic Church is clear on this matter."

"You helped the freedom fighters and I've heard you give sermons against apartheid. I don't understand why you won't help me with this! Jesus said, 'Whatsoever you do to the least of my brothers, so you do unto me.' Isn't this exactly what he meant?"

"Even if I agreed that it was the same thing, the Church won't allow it."

Grace imagined Bessy's broken face and blood rushed into her own and she almost spat in anger: "You're German, you of all people know what happens when you blindly obey orders."

While his face turned the color of red ants, Father Sebastian's eyes seemed to lose all their color and a thick vein popped out of his forehead. He opened his mouth but then closed it again and walked out without saying a word.

Shamu! Grace knew that she had gone too far. She knew that she was right, but just as Mrs. Njavwa had warned, being right wasn't worth a bunch of bananas. Mrs. Njavwa would be angry with her, and she in turn felt a rush of anger towards God. If we are all equal in your eyes, why not make us equal on earth? Why was life so difficult for some of your children, but not for others? She thought about Suzanna, the Londoners and Bwalya, who had everything without a single day of hardship. Why did she have to struggle so hard, and Bessy have it even harder? Grace stared at the wooden cross on Father Sebastian's wall, wishing God would explain himself.

That night Grace dreamt of fire. She found herself at the fork of the Nyakawise river, close to Mr. Patel's store but dressed for work in her suit and kitten heels. She felt annoyed that she would have to make the long trip back to Lusaka, but not unduly so because she could visit Mr. Patel and eat samosas on his veranda before she caught the bus. Grace hurried towards the store but then realized she was headed in the wrong direction and was even closer to the village. She turned around but the path behind her had been swallowed by a forest of strange msolo trees with branches that stretched all the way to the ground and were covered in long thorns. Grace tried to navigate through them but the thorns were as sharp as razors and ripped her suit and shredded her legs. Bending down to wipe the blood off, she noticed that one of her shoes was on fire. How did that happen? She tried to stamp it out, but the flames spread to the other one. Grace jumped out of her shoes and stomped them with her bare feet but the fire raged on, leaping from tree to tree. Although the fire didn't feel hot, it still burned; her shoes disintegrated into ash, her feet curled up like burnt leaves and the smoke became so thick that she couldn't see beyond her outstretched arms. Grace instinctively knew that she had to get to the river and so she closed her eyes and jumped as far as she could and somehow landed in the middle of the Nyakawise. The current swept her downstream as the cool water healed her burnt feet and her bleeding legs, and felt like balm on her naked skin. Wait! What happened to my suit? I can't go to work without a suit! Avaristo's going to kill me! She swore as she swam to the shore, slunk out of the water and hid her nakedness behind a boulder. Grace immediately recognized the configuration of the rocks—this big one was where she had cast out her bamboo fishing rod, and the medium one where she had hidden to spy on the boys splashing in the river, and the small one where she liked to sit watching quelea swarm in geometric shapes over the water at dusk. These rocks marked the westernmost territory of Nyamphande village. Before she could process how she got there, Grace heard a roar behind her. The fire had followed her to the village, or had it driven her back here? Naked and as helpless as a newborn, Grace was unable to move, to call out, or do anything but watch the flames burn everything to ash—huts, the small church, the mango trees, boulders and all the protective msolo trees. She knew that there was nothing left for the inferno to devour but her.

11

Grace waited at the Mingling Bar on campus. The cryptic note that "B" left at the office instructed her to meet there at 18:00 hours. Esther, who manned the reception when she wasn't gossiping, smoking outside or making tea, hadn't seen who left the note, but Grace figured it could only have been from Bwalya. The Mingling Bar a constellation of concrete benches and tables tucked into a hollow under the university's administration building, was the least romantic spot to meet on campus. She nonetheless felt excitement eddy through her at the thought of seeing Bwalya again. Maybe when it got dark they could stroll down to the university lake, where lovers often made out behind the weeping willows. She ran her hands over her braids to smooth down errant hairs and surreptitiously sniffed her armpits to make sure she had on enough deodorant to smell like an enchanted garden, as the canister promised.

The place felt different with all the students gone. She had read in the newspaper that the President had closed the university for two weeks due to the rioting over the cancellation of the scholarship program, and that the police had forcibly removed all students from campus. She knew how much poor students depended on it; her scholarship meant that she could stay in university without Mr. Patel's support, and that she could afford books and stationery, and even an occasional Fanta at the Mingling Bar. The usual bustle and frenetic movement on campus was absent, and all signs of the riots had been erased. The few people around all seemed to be rushing home, now that the sun was setting. She saw her former professor, Dr. Dzekedzeke, walking in her direction with a book bag in one hand and her cane in the other. She had been the first professor to encourage Grace to challenge what she was being taught. They delighted in sparring with each other, arguing the merits of a case back and forth. The professor had an encyclopedic knowledge of the law, so Grace would prepare for hours to try to best her. Today, anxious to meet Bwalya, she shrank into the shadows and stayed hidden until the professor had gone past.

Tired of standing, Grace sat down on a concrete bench. It felt cool and pleasant after a hot day. She looked out at the white rotunda of the library that seemed to glow in the dark. She missed university, and the library most of all. Grace had spent many happy hours in there; she would spiral up the circular ramp, find the book she was looking for and settle at her favorite desk that was bathed in warm sunlight pouring down through the skylights. That life, worrying about maintaining perfect A's to keep her scholarship, seemed a long time ago.

Grace didn't have a watch, but it was fully dark now so she figured it must be about 19:00 hours. Where was he? She vacillated between being worried and being annoyed. Maybe he had crashed his Fiat 127 into a tree. Maybe he was just running late. But what if he was dead in a ditch; or worse, what if he had stood her up!

Grace was about to give up and leave when Bwalya finally arrived. He apologized for being late, but offered no explanation. He looked around as if to confirm that they were alone before he sat down. He settled next to her, also facing outward, but his body language was completely different from their evening at Mr. Pete's. He didn't sit close to her, and there was no smiling, no flirting and no kissing. She suddenly felt embarrassed about all that kissing and groping in his Fiat outside of Mrs. Njavwa's gate after their dinner. If it wasn't for Goliath making a racket, barking and hurling himself against the metal gate, they might have gone further.

"The DPP filed a *nolle prosequi* in your case this morning," he said.

"What? He's not prosecuting Bessy anymore? That's wonderful!" Grace felt relieved to the point of delirium and laughed out loud and clapped. Finally, some good news. "Thank God! Willbess can go home!" She would take the *nolle* to the police station the minute she got her hands on it, so that Willbess wouldn't spend a moment longer in that prison. She would enjoy shoving it into Officer Lungu's face. She tried to hug Bwalya but he shook her off, and inched away.

"What's wrong?" She felt confused. What had happened between the last night they were together and today?

Bwalya looked furtive as he told Grace that he had seen Police Chief Sampa and the Attorney General go into the DPP's office. He explained that Chief Sampa was his father's friend and helped him get the job, so when he saw him, he hovered nearby to say hello and overheard them arguing.

"The Attorney General ended the argument by shouting that it was an order from on high, and that they had no choice. At that point, I snuck off. I didn't think much about it until later when the DPP called me into his office. He gave me some paperwork to take directly to Justice Mwendapole, and said to wait as long as it took for him to stamp it, then to return it directly to him, 'For his eyes only.' He said he trusted me because I was close to the Police Chief. I didn't know it was your case until I opened the envelope at court."

"I don't understand. What's the problem if they're letting Willbess go?"

He glanced at Grace before looking away again. "Yesterday the DPP was ready to hang your client, and now he can't drop the case fast enough? I know him, he's not one to back down easily, and neither is Chief Sampa."

Grace's mind began to race. "Do you think it's because Officer Lungu beat Willbess up?" Because of Avaristo's warning to wait until Bessy was out of prison, she hadn't filed a report against Lungu yet, but maybe word had gotten to the Police Chief that his officer had beaten a prisoner and roughed up a lawyer.

Bwalya made a face. "You can't be that naïve, Grace. The DPP wouldn't drop the charges over something so trivial. This troika isn't meeting unless something's very wrong."

"Something like what?"

Bwalya shrugged. "I've told you what I know, and more than I should've. And Grace, you can't tell anybody that we met."

"What about the room full of people at Mr. Pete's?" Grace smiled at him, hoping to rekindle the romance from that evening, and that a smile would replace the worried look on his face.

"I could lose my job if the DPP finds out that I talked to you, or that we're friends."

Friends? Grace felt like she had been kicked in the stomach.

"If you care about your career and maybe even your safety, you'll get as far away from this thing as you can."

"Just so it's clear, Bwalya, I'd never turn my back on my client."

"It's a lost cause, Grace. Save yourself."

Bwalya stood up and walked away. Grace watched him leave, trying in vain to think of something to say to get him to come back. He wouldn't leave me here alone in the dark, she thought, moments before seeing his Fiat speed away. Shamu! What a fool I must be for falling for such a tardy, cowardly, stupid donkey!

Grace walked back to the main road with her shoulders hunched over, her hands in her jacket pockets and her head bowed as though pushing against a strong wind. The sun had been a golden orb in the sky when she'd raced up this same street to meet Bwalya, and she had been smiling as brightly as the shimmering lake. Now the road back was a mosaic of darkness and shadows, the lake a pit of molten tar, and the willows shape-shifting monsters reaching for her with long tentacles. Grace picked up her pace and then broke into a jog, and kept running until she got to the well-lit main road where she waited for a bus. As long as Will-bess gets out of jail, she thought, who cares about Bwalya. The wind picked up and Grace smelled rain in the air. She looked up at the night sky and could see dark clouds gathering between her and the waning moon. Shamu! That's all I need right now. Grace wrapped her arms around herself and blinked back tears.

12

It was the third night that Grace wasn't able to sleep. First it was the storm. Fierce wind thrashed through the trees and lightning crashed down from the sky, momentarily exposing the spirit world. The frangipani tree outside her window banged and scratched as if trying to escape to the inside. After the thunderstorm petered out, she still couldn't sleep. She pulled the covers up over her shoulders, then she felt too hot and pushed them down to her waist; she shifted her pillow and lay on her stomach for a while, then tried rolling onto her back. She sighed and gave up. It had taken two days of waiting before the *nolle prosequi* arrived at her office after-hours. She was working late and took it home with her so that she could go to the police station first thing the next morning. She was worried about Will-bess. Why had Bwalya been so spooked? What did he mean that the case was a lost cause? She hoped the police hadn't hurt Bessy again. I'll find out tomorrow, she thought, but worried more and more as the rain drummed on and the shadows paced across the ceiling until morning.

At dawn, Grace got out of bed and put on her suit. She stood at the window fully dressed but still barefoot, and pressed her head against the cold glass, watching and willing the rain to stop. She considered going to the police station anyway but the rain was too heavy and she didn't have an umbrella.

It was another long hour before it finally stopped. Grace scanned the pewter sky and saw a distant patch of blue blossoming fast enough to tell her that the rain was done. The frangipani nodded and shook raindrops off its waxy leaves, so she slipped on her shoes, grabbed her bag and ran out of the front door.

She arrived at the police station just after eight in the morning. Because of the downpour, there were only a few people milling around. A street vendor with banana fritters stuffed into a bucket held one up and waved it enticingly at Grace. It looked crispy and delicious and her stomach growled. She hadn't eaten in her hurry to get Willbess out, but she needed all her money to get him home by taxi. She worried that Avaristo would dispute her reimbursement claim; she hadn't cleared it prior and he was particularly fussy with pro bono cases where expenses couldn't be passed on to the client. She hop-scotched across the muddy puddles in the pavement before running up the clean, rain-swept white stairway. When she saw police boots sticking out from under the desk in the foyer, she thought it was

Officer Lungu and stopped so suddenly that she skidded on the slick stairs. She hadn't seen the policeman since he had shoved her to the ground and knocked her out. Taking a moment to recover, she imagined the Mulenga family hugging Willbess, crying and laughing with joy, and willed her feet forward, balling up her left fist before she walked in. Officer Lungu won't catch me off-guard; I'll punch him in the potbelly if he touches me again.

Grace felt a rush of relief. It was a different policeman behind the mukwa desk and this one looked like the antithesis of Lungu. He was perfectly neat in a crisp uniform, with an angular face and high cheekbones softened by a pouty mouth and a crown of red hair, parted and brushed down in waves around his head. His skin was a hint lighter than his khaki uniform. Grace thought of Suzanna and how she admired beautiful men—not that she would ever date a policeman. She would lament pretty boys who she declared un-dateable due to their lower class, and shrug off Grace's indignation: "I'm only being honest!" Grace would never date a policeman either, but for different reasons. Based on her experience, they were all tainted. As if to affirm her suspicion, Grace noticed that this policeman's smooth skin was marred by a bad scar on his neck, just above his shirt collar. He looked like he had survived an attack from a leopard.

"I'm from DB & Associates and I'm here to collect my client," Grace said. The policeman didn't bother to look up from reading the newspaper laid out on the desk. Officer Lungu's messy folders were now all gone, and there was nothing to obscure the view. Grace pulled the court order out of her bag and placed it on top of the paper. The policeman looked up in annoyance, his eyes a striking green color. Grace held his gaze. She wasn't going to be intimidated.

"This is a *nolle prosequi*, an order of the court that mandates that you release my client, Willbess Mulenga, forthwith."

He handed it back to her without looking at it. "There is a bench around the corner, go there and wait with the other women *forthwith*." He licked his index finger and turned the page of the newspaper.

"I said I'm here to collect my client and I'm not waiting."

The policeman lifted his newspaper up between them. Grace resisted the urge to smack it down.

"Do I need to report you to Police Chief Sampa?" She didn't try to keep the edge out of her voice, she was sick of these policemen.

He put down the newspaper and looked at her again as if to reassess her. "Only authorized personnel allowed up there," he finally replied. He sounded dismissive but Grace saw hesitation flicker in his green eyes, and he didn't raise his newspaper again.

"Which way to Police Chief Sampa's office?"

"You can't go up there," he said, looking briefly to the left. Grace remembered a narrow stairway from the day she had followed Officer Lungu down that same corridor and started walking in that direction, hoping it was the right way.

"Iwe! You get back here!" The officer stood up, shouting at her back.

Grace raced down the corridor and then up the stairs, taking two at a time. If the policeman was following her, he was going to have to sprint to catch her. At the top of the stairs she paused, looked back and listened. No footsteps. *Good.* Unlike the dark, labyrinthine corridors in the lower bowels of the police station, this floor had one corridor with large windows at both ends flooding in light that bounced off the white walls and polished floor. There were only two office doors, one on each side of the corridor. The door on the left was marked "Chief of Police." Grace knocked and immediately walked in. She found a room with white walls, a metal desk and the typewriter were also white, as was the air conditioner that hummed as it blew cold air into the office. An elderly woman was at the desk speaking into a phone cradled into her shoulder while she pecked at the typewriter in front of her. The woman's hair was elaborately braided like a nest of silver snakes on top of her head. She smiled at Grace, pointed at a small maroon loveseat in the corner and continued her conversation. Its maroon velour looked incongruous, an unseemly red gash in an otherwise austere white room. Grace sat on the edge of the loveseat and looked around, pretending not to listen.

"Why do you even want him out of prison, he's a *useless* chap!" The woman listened for a minute and rested her fingers on the typewriter keys. She shook her grey head, and rolled her eyes. She lowered her voice. "Okay, my dear,

I'll help you but don't forget that thing we discussed." She paused and listened again before replying in almost a hiss, "Of course not! Bring it to my house."

The door opened and a man in uniform walked in. His khaki shirt was adorned with gold buttons down the front and gold medallions on the lapels, and his cap had golden brocade on the brim. He looked formal despite his uniform's short sleeves. The woman hung up the phone immediately and stood up.

"Good morning, Chief Sampa, sir." Grace thought she was going to salute.

He nodded. "Mrs. Lupupa." When he saw Grace, he cocked his capped head and frowned at Mrs. Lupupa.

"She's trying to make an appointment with you, sir. I was just telling her that you are too busy," Mrs. Lupupa lied. Grace noticed her wringing her hands.

The man nodded and tried to hurry past. He opened an adjoining door that led into a large office. Grace saw her chance, leapt up and followed him in.

Chief Sampa wasn't very tall but he was lean and strong, and his arms bulged under his short sleeves as he took the cap off his clean-shaven head. He did not look happy but he motioned for Grace to sit on the other side of his desk before he sat down himself. To the right of the desk was the rest of the maroon velour set, two single chairs and a couch with a low coffee table in the middle. Behind him was a bookshelf, but in place of books were rows of gold and silver trophies, many with tiny shiny men in judogi in various poses. Grace noticed a framed certificate also displayed prominently: "International Judo Federation Dan, 3rd Black, awarded to Mubanga Sampa."

Mrs. Lupupa stood in the doorway. She cleared her throat and asked, "Some tea, sir?"

"No. Close the door, please." Chief Sampa's voice was low and gravelly and he spoke softly, making him hard to understand. Grace imagined police officers standing in formation, straining to figure out Chief Sampa's commands. He sat down and turned his gaze to Grace. "Yes?" He didn't sound unfriendly but his small black eyes and intent stare unsettled her. Grace briefly explained who she was, and handed him the court order. Chief Sampa barely glanced at it before he gave it back.

"You should have saved yourself a trip. Mr. Willbess Mulenga was released yesterday."

Grace wasn't expecting that. "Yesterday? Are you sure?" Her mind raced. Could Willbess be home already? The Mulengas didn't have a phone so they wouldn't have had a chance to call her. Chief Sampa stood up but Grace didn't move.

She remembered what Bwalya had said about the meeting of the troika and knew something was wrong, she felt it.

"If there's nothing else...?" The Police Chief looked at his watch, a heavy gold piece that clinked when he twisted his wrist.

"My firm only received a copy of the order from the DPP's office after-hours yesterday."

"And?"

"It's unusual for the DPP to send an order directly to the police station, isn't it?"

"No."

Grace knew he was lying. It wasn't only unusual, it was unheard of. Lawyers brought the orders to the police station, and the police enjoyed jerking them around for hours before they would release a prisoner. Chief Sampa marched to the door and held it open.

"I want copies of the release paperwork."

"Leave your details with Mrs. Lupupa, and she will have them sent to your firm as soon as possible. Now, if you'll excuse me, I have important matters to attend to."

He instructed Mrs. Lupupa through the open door to help her. As soon as Grace reached the door-frame, he closed it, effectively pushing her out of his office.

Grace handed the court order to Mrs. Lupupa, who wrote down the details on what looked like the back of an old letter.

"When will I get the paperwork?" Grace asked, reading Mrs. Lupupa's notes upside down to confirm that she had copied all the information correctly.

"You heard the Police Chief." She handed Grace back the order.

"When exactly?"

"As he said, pangono, pangono."

"Mrs. Lupupa, do you know anything more about this case?"

The silver snakes on Mrs. Lupupa's head shook slightly. "Me? I'm just a secretary. I don't know anything."

Grace noticed that Mrs. Lupupa was wringing her hands again and wouldn't look her in the eye.

13

The Mulenga house in Kalikiliki appeared empty except for the yellow dog. This time Munali remembered Grace and didn't bark or growl, instead escorting her to the front door wagging her tail. Grace knocked hard a few times and called out "Odi?" When no one answered, she sat on the single stair to the house, petting the yellow dog while she waited. "Hello, Munali," she said to the dog, who shook with excitement. Anytime Grace tried to stop, the dog pushed its oversized head under her hand, compelling her to continue petting until finally the dog yawned, curled into a ball under Grace's legs and fell asleep. Grace yawned too. She leaned back with her arms stretched behind her and her long legs in front of her, willing Bessy to appear in the gap in the hedge. Instead, a man on a bicycle with a goat tied to the back cycled past, and then a woman walked past with a large bag of charcoal on her head and pulling

a little girl along behind her. A few minutes later, a young
woman in a short green dress and red heels picked her way
across the gravel, followed by a dour-looking man in a Father Christmas suit and cotton-wool beard who stomped
past in gumboots. After a long lull, a gaggle of teenagers
laughing woke the dog up. Munali ran out and chased them
back in the direction that they had come from. When the
dog reappeared, she was with Loveness.

Loveness stopped in her tracks when she saw Grace, who
stood up, dusted herself off and swiped at the dog's short
golden hairs sticking to the front of her skirt.

"Down!" Loveness shouted at the dog yapping and paw-
ing the air next to her, then turned to Grace. "Ba Mayo will
be home soon. It's best she doesn't find you here." As she
spoke, Loveness took a few steps back into the gap in the
bougainvillea hedge and scanned the road for her mother.

"Did Bessy come back home yesterday?"

Loveness turned back. "No," she replied, almost as a
question. "We were at the prison yesterday, and the police
told us to come back today. Ba Mayo's there again."

"Is there anywhere else Bessy would go? I mean, if he
didn't want to come home." Grace thought about Mrs.
Mulenga's violent reaction to Willbess being charged with
having sex with another man.

Loveness's eyes narrowed. "He'd come straight home.
Why?"

"The police said they released him yesterday."

Loveness shook her head. "We were there yesterday, we
sat on that bench the whole day! Ba Mayo's been there every

single day for months now, and she'll keep going until they release Bessy. We've been praying that he'd make it home in time for Christmas tomorrow, but it doesn't look like it'll happen." Loveness looked at the dying sun. "Ba Mayo should be on her way from the prison right now."

"Are you sure there's nowhere else Bessy could've gone?"

"He has nowhere to go. He had a boyfriend once, but that ended a long time ago."

"What's this boyfriend's name?"

Loveness shrugged. "Bessy called him 'Darling.' He said that they were going to escape to a place called San Frisco where they could be together openly. Is that a real place?"

Grace thought about what Suzanna had said about the gay bars in London. "I don't know San Frisco, but I've heard of other places. Does your mother know about Bessy?"

"He doesn't hide it. Ba Mayo knows but she doesn't understand. I can't say I understand myself, but he's always been like this and I can't imagine him any other way. When we were little, we'd both wear dresses and tell people that we were twin girls, like Agnes and Eneless, and everyone believed us." Grace could see how they would easily pass as twin girls. The resemblance was striking, the same almond-shaped face, delicate features and big eyes—Loveness, the undamaged version. "Ba Mayo made him stop but we'd still do it when my parents weren't home." Loveness smiled at the memory but then her smile faded. "He said his darling really understood him and encouraged him to be himself. That's when he stopped hiding and started dressing like a girl all the time. He got expelled from school for wearing a skirt, and you can imagine the chaos at home. My mother even brought in an exorcist." Loveness laughed without mirth. "When that didn't work, Ba Mayo started telling her church friends that Bessy's a comedian and wears dresses to make people laugh. I know it hurts him, but he never contradicts her, or gets angry when her stupid friends make fun of him. I guess that's how they manage. To be so close, that is. Despite it all, Bessy's always been her favorite. I think she's more afraid for him than anything else. He's been beaten up more times than I can count, and now this."

"So what happened to the guy?"

"His boyfriend? He got married. Bessy was completely devastated. Before that, he'd been so happy, talking about how they would elope and get married in America."

"I don't think that men can marry each other, even in America." It occurred to Grace that while she had had to fight *not* to get married, others would have to fight *to* get married. Same-sex marriage could never happen in Zambia in her lifetime, of that Grace was sure, but maybe one day the laws would change in other more progressive countries, and then eventually it would have to happen here too.

"Well, Bessy believed that they could. In fact that's all he talked about before he found out that his darling got married to a girl. Imagine, he didn't even have the decency to tell Bessy; my brother had to read about it in the paper."

"Must be a prominent person if he was in the newspaper. Did you see the announcement? Do you remember any names?"

Loveness shook her head. "I didn't see it. I just remember how much Bessy cried." Loveness's eyes watered as she spoke. "He was depressed for months and then one day he said to hell with his ex, he'd get himself to America." Munali stood up again and moved closer. Loveness put her hand on the dog's big head. "Bessy joked that at least he got custody of their dog. He even tried to change her name to Sweetness, but the dog was already used to Munali and wouldn't respond."

"Do you know anything more about this man? Did Bessy meet him at the MacGyver?"

"I don't think so. Bessy only started going there after they broke up." Loveness sat down on the stair, placed her face in her hands and her elbows on her knees. "I know he wasn't just dancing, he was doing bad things to make money. Once Bessy had made up his mind, he was going to get to America no matter the cost. I begged him to stop but he wouldn't listen to me. I even followed him to the MacGyver, but the giant bouncer there threatened me and I never went back. You have to understand, he's desperate."

Grace did understand. She remembered standing under the msolo tree on the bank of the Nyakawise ready to drown herself in the river.

"Something bad has happened to him, I can feel it," Loveness whispered. The dog seemed to sense it as well and began whimpering. When Loveness looked up, Grace noticed that she was crying. Munali licked her face, and Loveness embraced the dog. Grace crouched down to comfort Loveness.

"What are you doing here?"

Grace turned and saw Mrs. Mulenga standing over her.

She had been so focused on Loveness that she hadn't heard her come into the yard. She stood up quickly and took a step back to create more distance between them.

"I'm only here because the police said they released Bessy—I mean Willbess. I came to check if he was here."

"Is he here?" Mrs. Mulenga asked Loveness, her eyes alight until Loveness shook her head.

"Then where is he?" Mrs. Mulenga asked Grace.

"I don't know."

"You don't know?" Mrs. Mulenga sneered at her. "What is the point of a lawyer who doesn't know anything?"

"I'm doing my best."

"Your best? You've done nothing for him. You can't even tell me where he is!"

Mrs. Mulenga was right, it didn't matter if Grace was trying her best when it didn't yield results. She didn't know what else she could've done, what else she could still do, or what to say to Mrs. Mulenga who was glowering at her. "My apologies for disturbing you. The police said they had released Willbess so I came here to check."

"Apologies? My son disappears and that's all you have to say? Who are you anyway? Where did you come from? I don't want you here. I want my son!"

Grace recognized that expression on Mrs. Mulenga's face. It was the same look as the last time she erupted. Veins ran down her forehead and her face seemed pulled by a centripetal force behind her angry eyes. Grace made to leave but Mrs. Mulenga blocked her and pushed her back. As an

automatic response, Grace raised her fists as her father had
shown her.

"You're not leaving until you tell me where my son is."
Mrs. Mulenga glared at Grace, her chest rising and falling.

Shamu! Am I going to have to fight this woman? Grace
thought.

Mrs. Mulenga lurched at her and Grace blocked and parried, but Mrs. Mulenga managed to grab her jacket as she
went down. Grace fell, and she kept falling without hitting
the ground. She knew immediately what was happening.
It had been a long time, so long that her anyina had declared her cured, *praise Jesus!* Not since her father's funeral
and the first time she understood that something strange
and powerful was happening to her.

It had been the rainy season and roiling dark clouds
threatened another downpour. Too muddy to sit down, the
whole village stood in a loose circle around the grave. The
priest kept scanning the sky as he rushed through Grace's
father's funeral service. When he finished, he made the sign
of the cross over her atate's coffin and six young men lowered the casket into the grave using thick vines. Grace kept
her eyes fixed on the priest's hem to avoid seeing her father
go into that dark hole. She watched the black material en-
crusted with red mud sway when the priest moved. As was
the tradition at funerals, the women cried "Ye-e-egh!" and
the male mourners responded "Pamvwika kulila!" and then
the church choir joined in with a mournful dirge. Two of
the young men began to shovel earth into the grave. Grace
winced at the sound of the mud clumps hitting the wooden

coffin. Then she heard her father call her name. She remembered being confused; he was dead and being buried in a cheap wooden coffin right in front of her eyes, yet she heard his voice loud and clear. Then she felt herself falling. This had happened often when she was a child, but it felt different this time, she had never felt pain before, not even when she hit concrete or stones, but this time the pain was excruciating. She felt her body being pulled then twisted in opposing directions. Grace was being ripped apart and her last thought before she passed out was that she would die too.

When she had come to, Mr. Patel, covered in mud himself, was carrying her into her mother's hut. Grace was surprised to find that all of her pain had disappeared and been replaced with a feeling of clarity and power, euphoria even, as she knew that her father had successfully crossed over to become her ancestor. In that moment, Grace suddenly understood that what she had experienced during childhood wasn't the affliction they called njilinjili; she was a wamizimu, someone with the powers of direct connection to the ancestors.

Now, in the Mulengas' yard, Grace didn't remember hitting the ground, but had the sensation that she was upright. She wiggled her toes but still couldn't feel anything. She had trouble opening her eyes but when she did, there it was. It wasn't large or imposing, or at all frightening. Rather, its shiny gold coat and black spots across its face and down its back were mesmerizing. She knew that only the most powerful ngangas had powers strong enough to see the spirit escort, but there it was. The leopard looked back at Grace with its intense yellow eyes and pin-prick pupils, and switched its tail a few times. With each flick, currents pulsed across the ndembo on her face and down her back. She felt it was trying to explain many things that she couldn't decipher, but she did understand one thing with clarity, that Bessy had crossed over.

She blinked again and there were clouds above her. It took Grace a minute to realize that she was lying on a bed in a room with an azure ceiling decorated with nimbus clouds created using a thick white paint. She could hear Agnes, Eneless and Loveness talking about her. Grace turned her head to look around the room while the sisters argued. Each wall was painted a different color except the wall closest to her which was covered with an artistic mosaic of hundreds of magazine clippings.

"What if she dies? People die from epilepsy all the time."

"No, they don't, Loveness."

"Yeah, you don't know what you're talking about, Loveness. Ba Mayo barely touched her anyway." The twins agreed that if it was anyone's fault, it was Grace's for trespassing.

"If she survives, she could sue Ba Mayo for attacking her and triggering the seizure."

Grace heard the twins suck their teeth at Loveness. "She's our lawyer, she can't sue Ba Mayo."

"Of course she can't sue us, dummy."

"She's not our lawyer, she's Bessy's. Hey, look! Ene, Aggie, her eyes are open!" They all turned to stare at Grace.

"Hello," was all Grace could think to say.

"Loveness, get Ba Mayo," said one twin. "Hurry!" said the other.

★ ★ ★

Mrs. Mulenga instructed her daughters to leave. She remained standing a short distance from the bed and said, "I didn't know that you're epileptic. It's no excuse but I haven't been myself since…" Mrs. Mulenga trailed off.

Grace raised herself up to her elbows and was surprised at the tears that fell out of her eyes. She sat up completely, wiped her face and swung her feet to the floor. Her mind felt clear and her body powerful. "I'm not epileptic. It just looks like njilinjili but it's not. I'm fine, perfectly fine."

Mrs. Mulenga looked doubtful. "I shouldn't have grabbed you. I'm sorry."

Grace found her shoes placed neatly next to the bed and pushed her feet into them. "It's okay."

"No, nothing is okay." Mrs. Mulenga covered her mouth with one hand and held her stomach with the other. "My son's no more! I know it!" Mrs. Mulenga collapsed in Grace's arms like she had no bones and it felt strangely comfortable to hold her. Eventually Mrs. Mulenga gathered herself and was able to sit more upright but she stayed in Grace's arms. "It's not just the way the police have been acting these last weeks; they practically run at the sight of me. I'm his mother and I can't feel him here anymore. I can't explain it any better but I know my only son is gone." At that, Mrs. Mulenga began to weep.

Grace couldn't explain to Mrs. Mulenga that she also knew that Bessy was now an ancestor. Instead she said, "I also felt it when my father crossed over," and remembering the blond Jesus hanging in the living room she added, "to heaven." Wasn't it the same place? Was it?

Mrs. Mulenga began to rock back and forth and Grace swayed with her. "How do I tell my husband? And what about my poor girls? How will we survive?" Grace thought about her own family. She had never seen it herself, but her father said they had been happy once upon a time, that theirs was a love match and not an arranged marriage. Grace knew that everything went wrong after they buried Joy, her eldest sibling. She didn't have the heart to tell Mrs. Mulenga that in her experience families didn't survive the death of a child. As if she heard Grace's thoughts, Mrs. Mulenga began to wail so loudly that within seconds the twins and Loveness burst in. They looked confused at the sight of their mother in Grace's arms, but joined to form a protective cone around her.

"No need for tears, my child. So we disagreed. So you missed Christmas mass yesterday. *Alles gut.* All is forgiven." Grace shook her head and buried herself more deeply into Father Sebastian's massive frame. The priest had misunderstood her sudden reappearance at his office; Grace *was* sorry for what she had said to him, or, to be more precise, how she had said it, but these tears were for Bessy.

"They killed him! He's dead! Bessy's dead!" Grace managed to say while still clinging on to the priest. He patted her back gently until she had gathered herself, and then sat her down with a box of tissues that he had handy for such occasions. She pulled a few out of the box and blew her nose while shaking her head, then used a clean corner to wipe her eyes.

"Who's Bessy?"

"My client. Willbess Mulenga, the one I told you about."

"Who killed him? What happened? Did you go to the police?"

"The police killed him! I can't prove it, but it was the police."

"Tell me what happened, my child."

Grace tried to tell the priest everything but Father Sebastian interrupted her. "Wamizimu? You mean that superstitious nonsense?"

"It's not superstition at all." Grace tried to explain but the more she talked about the trance, the fits that resembled epilepsy and the visions, the more it did sound like a foolish superstition.

Father Sebastian wagged a finger at her. "*Na komm,* Grace, you're an educated woman now, you can't still believe in this mumbo jumbo."

She felt insulted. Grace had always found the old priest's inflexibility towards the spirit world baffling. He accepted angels and the Holy Spirit but rejected outright ancestors and any other spirits as pagan superstitions. This seemed illogical to her; either you believed in spirits or you didn't. "It's more than belief, it's been my experience and what I know to be true." She touched her face, feeling the cicatrices under her fingertips. "If anything, it's my belief in God that's shaken."

Grace had once felt close to God. In the village, her

mother had instructed her to feel his warmth through the soil under her feet, see his protection in the sheltering sky above and witness his power in the Nyakawise river after the rains. Even at her lowest, watching her father die a miserable death, Grace never doubted God. It was his will and Grace had faith in his plan, even if she didn't understand it. At university, things began to change for her; she learned to question everything, including God. She asked him questions. Why the poverty and suffering? Why starvation and disease? And now, with Bessy's death, she wanted answers. Why let him die alone in a filthy prison? He was just a boy! It wasn't that she stopped believing entirely, but she demanded answers. Blind faith wasn't good enough anymore.

"This case has raised so many questions, and I ask God and he won't answer me." Even before she had seen the leopard with her own eyes, she always felt her ancestors when they were close, and felt that they tried to communicate with her directly or indirectly through ngangas. God didn't even seem to try, and his silence angered her. "I'm not sure what God's doing up there, if he's up there at all."

Father Sebastian pulled his chair closer to her, held her gaze and both her hands. "The Bible says *Trust in the Lord with all thine heart; and lean not unto thine own understanding. In all thy ways acknowledge him, and he shall direct thy paths.*"

"I know what the Bible says. I've read it cover to cover and I want to believe, Father, I do, but I'm having a really hard time with God right now."

"I know it's not always easy, but faith isn't meant to be easy. It's normal to question and have doubts."

"Have you?"

"Of course! Faith isn't constant for any human. And we priests are just humans after all."

Grace was shocked; it hadn't occurred to her that a priest could have doubts. It felt like a revelation. "You've doubted God's existence?"

"No, my child, I have no doubt about God at all. I doubt myself. I'm near the end of my journey and I have doubts that I have fulfilled his purpose for me. Today I know my purpose is to help you with your faith. Whatever you might feel in the moment, know in your heart that God is with you." The priest looked up at the ceiling as if God was hovering by the rafters, then slipped off his seat and knelt facing the cross on the wall. "Let's pray." He put his hands together and waited for Grace to kneel next to him before he recited the Lord's prayer. Grace was distracted by the array of Christmas cards adorning the priest's office. Whatever did snow, pine trees, sleds, reindeer and old fat white men in red have to do with Christ's birth?

"Amen," Father Sebastian said finally.

"Amen," Grace echoed. She envied his absolute faith, but being close to the priest didn't provide answers, or make her feel any closer to God. She couldn't feel his presence at all. In truth, she felt nothing but the hard parquet floor against her knees and was glad to stand up again.

Father Sebastian seemed to sense that Grace needed more. "When I'm stuck, I go to the Bible. I start at Genesis and keep reading until I find the answer. In starting from the

beginning, I always discover new things that I missed before."

Grace nodded but she wasn't thinking about her father's
Bible that lay long unopened on her bedside table. She
was thinking about the beginning of the case. Back to the
MacGyver. Who was the man who had attacked Bessy? He
was the missing link between the bar fight and Bessy's arrest. Maybe he was the one who knew Bessy well enough
to direct the police to his house? Godfredah had believed
that they knew each other. He'd also mentioned that Mr.
MacGyver was looking for the guys to pay for the damage to his club. Maybe he had found them by now. Grace
needed to find the bar owner.

14

A man in overalls stacking crates of beer onto a juddering truck directed Grace to the back of the warehouse. She walked down the dark corridor between crates of Mosi beer and blue-and-white boxes marked "Absolutely Vodka." At the back, Grace found a huge man sitting behind a make-shift desk cobbled together from an old door balanced across empty Mosi crates. He was tapping expertly on a calculator with his left index finger as he moved his right down a column of numbers in a ledger book. His fingernails were long and filed to sharp points, like claws on a bird of prey. In spite of the dress-shirt and tie, Grace recognized the small peanut-shaped head atop that enormous body.

"Big Daddy?"

Big Daddy closed the ledger book even before he looked up. He eyed Grace for a few moments, closed his eyes, raking through his salt-and-pepper goatee with his claws, and then popped them open again. "You're one of the girls from the club."

"Grace Zulu, the lawyer representing Willbess Mulenga."

"A lawyer?" Big Daddy raised his eyebrows. "What can I do for you, Lawyer Grace?"

"I need information."

"Well you've come to the wrong place. *Absolutely* the wrong place." Big Daddy pointed at a box of vodka and chuckled at his own joke, revealing crooked brown teeth. "My business interests require utmost discretion. Indeed, Discretion is my middle name. Madaliso Discretion Mwanamambo." He made a zipping motion with his fingers against his fleshy lips and his eyes disappeared into his cheeks. "How did you find me, eh?" he asked. He had stopped smiling.

"The City Council Liquor Licensing office. You're listed as the owner of both the MacGyver Bar and this place, Spirited Distributors. I was looking for a Mr. Mwanamambo; I really didn't expect to find you, Big Daddy."

"Big Daddy's my street name. Tell me, where are my entertainers, Bessy and Godfredah?"

"I don't know about Godfredah, but Bessy's dead." Grace watched his response carefully. She was certain from his expression that this was news to him, bad news.

"What happened?" Big Daddy was clawing his goatee again, this time aggressively.

"He disappeared in police custody. They killed him. I mean, I can't prove it so I should say I believe they killed him."

Big Daddy slammed the table. "Mujeggas!"

Ndithu, Grace thought, mujegga is the right swearword for the police. "Godfredah said the men that were fighting in the club were doing some sort of karate. The police are trained in judo, so I'm thinking that those men could've been police. What do you think?"

"I think I pay a lot of kwacha to keep the police away from my establishments."

"The police picked up Bessy from his home after the fight, so someone must have known where he lived. If I can find that man, I'll be closer to finding who killed Bessy. Mr. Mwanamambo, do you know anything, or anyone who could help me?"

Big Daddy sat silently and stared at his calculator, as if adding up the cost of helping Grace. He nodded, grabbed his ledger book and ripped a page out of the back. "I'll write down the names of some suspects for you. Do you have a pen?" He stood up and opened a large hand with his palm up.

Grace began to fish for a pen in her bag. "I'm thinking that maybe you could come with me to the police station. You might recognize someone there. It's a bit of a long shot, but it would be worth the—"

Before she could finish her sentence, Big Daddy had grabbed her arm, twisted it behind her back and shoved her against the wall. She screamed, gurgling in pain as her face scraped against the rough concrete and he jerked her arm up hard. Big Daddy pressed his huge belly against her.

"Shout louder. Call for help!" he shouted himself.

"Help! Help me!" Grace continued to scream to the man in overalls outside. Her shouts reverberated off the tin roof, and Grace was sure that the man would hear the commotion and come running.

"Now shut up! Shut up!" Big Daddy slammed Grace against the wall several times until she shut up. Her body shook involuntarily and her arm felt like it would snap. Where the hell was the man in overalls? Big Daddy began to scratch her neck, at first gently and then, when Grace tried to squirm away, he dug his claws deep into her skin. Pain shot across her neck and throat, and she felt blood trickling down her neck. She worried about bloodstains on her white shirt, then panicked about her jugular being punctured. She started to cry, she didn't want to die in this ugly warehouse.

"Please don't kill me," Grace begged. How could she have been so stupid to come here alone. No one even knew where she was.

"Eh? If I wanted to kill you, you'd already be dead, dead, dead! No, Lawyer Grace, I'm going to help you. I'll teach you what they failed to at your fancy law school. Let's call them the laws of the jungle." Big Daddy chuckled and Grace felt his stomach shake against her back. He lowered Grace's arm slightly so it didn't hurt as much, but kept her pinned to the wall. He was heavy and Grace could hardly breathe. He spoke in her ear as though whispering secrets, and she could smell cigarettes on his breath. "Law number one, know who's on your side. You know that man outside who you were calling to help you? I pay him so he's on my side, not yours. You understand?"

Grace nodded, even though she had no idea what he was talking about, she just wanted to get out of there. She began to struggle desperately under the crush of Big Daddy, but he yanked her arm up again until she stopped moving. He released it a little.

"Law number two, no body, no crime. And there are so many ways to get rid of a body. You can dissolve it in acid, feed it to crocs in the Kafue river, throw it down the abandoned mineshafts in Kabwe…but it's not easy work. These policemen are lazy chaps; they probably dumped Bessy somewhere stupid, but even so, I doubt you'll find his body. And third, don't underestimate your enemies. See my big tummy?" He let go of Grace's arm and raised both hands, but kept her pinned down with his belly. Grace wedged her arms under her and tried with all her strength to lift him off her, but couldn't. Big Daddy slammed her with his stomach and knocked the air out of her. "Stop that and listen, eh? People look at me and see a fat pig, and don't realize until it's too late that I can pin down a man and rip out his throat in less than a minute." He showed Grace his long sharpened fingernails, now tipped with her blood. Grace started to shake again. "I'm not your enemy, Lawyer Grace. Your enemy is much more powerful than me. Bessy underestimated them and look what has happened. I told him that we have to be careful, discreet, hidden from this society that hates us…but he wouldn't listen. I hope you do when I tell you to leave this alone and don't make things any worse than they are." Big Daddy sighed deeply. When he spoke again, his voice sounded different, softer. "Bessy would always say, 'If we hide who we are, they'll never accept us. They're just scared of the unknown, but all people have goodness in their hearts, even you, Big Daddy,' and he'd try to hug me. Can you imagine such foolishness? Ahh, I'm going to miss that boy." Big Daddy stepped away and as soon as his weight was off her back, Grace flew down the corridor and escaped into the light.

Mrs. Mulenga had come unannounced again to DB & Associates. Grace found her in the conference room where Esther had asked her to wait. The room was designed to impress: high ceilings, track lighting, a polished ebony table that ran down the length of the room, twenty swivel chairs made of soft chocolate-brown leather arranged in perfect symmetry, rosewood shelves full of heavy tomes carrying the laws of the land and one giant abstract painting by a Nigerian artist that Avaristo name-dropped often, but Grace could never remember. She was grateful to find that Esther had brought Mrs. Mulenga tea in the bone-China set reserved for clients, and given her extra shortbread biscuits served on a tiny plate with a paper doily. If Mrs. Mulenga felt out of place in her chitenge and dusty plastic shoes, she didn't show it. She poured herself another cup of tea with a generous helping of milk and heaps of sugar. She handed Grace a biscuit before putting the rest in a handkerchief and placing them carefully in her handbag.

"What's our next move, Grace?"

"I'm sorry, Mrs. Mulenga, but nothing has changed. As I explained last time, without new evidence my hands are tied." She didn't mention that she was fighting Avaristo just to keep the file open. Once closed, the files were moved to gather dust in a storage unit outside of town.

"Here." Mrs. Mulenga pulled out a shoe box that she had in her lap, placed it on the table and slid it to Grace. "Open it." Grace hesitated, heeding the ransom-note assemblage of letters glued to the top of the box that read "Private. Do not open. This means you." There was a hand-drawn picture of a skull and crossbones underneath the warning.

"It's okay, it's Bessy's." Mrs. Mulenga nodded, so Grace opened the box slowly. In it she found a stack of kwacha in all denominations pinned to a quotation from a travel agent that itemized a one-way ticket on Zambian Airways from Lusaka to San Francisco for 2,500 kwacha. Underneath the money was a postcard of a red bridge suspended over turquoise water leading to a body of land almost lost in mist. Grace flipped it over but it was blank on the other side. She sifted through the rest of the miscellaneous objects in the box: a roll-on lip gloss; magazine clippings of a man wearing various hats, heavy make-up and ribbons in his long hair; a piece of white lace pinned to a pencil sketch of a wedding dress; and at the very bottom, a gold band with a diamond. Grace lifted the ring out of the box and held it up so that the gem caught the light.

"That's fake but the money is real," Mrs. Mulenga said. "Almost two thousand kwacha. I want you to use it to keep the case going."

Grace returned the ring to the box and closed it. "I could never take this money, Mrs. Mulenga. And you know it's not about money. The law is about what one can prove and I'm so sorry to have to put it to you this way, but without a body, I can't prove that they killed Bessy and our case can't move forward." She held Mrs. Mulenga's hand. "Unfortunately, these are the limitations of the law that we have to accept."

"I've had to accept many hard things, Grace. My son's dead because I failed him when he was alive. I cared so much about what other people thought that I wanted to change him instead of trying to understand him or even protect him. I can't fail him again. Please, if we give up now, my son would've died for nothing."

Grace would have felt better if Mrs. Mulenga had exploded as she had before. Instead she was calm and held on to Grace's hand with both of hers. Grace could feel everything Mrs. Mulenga felt, and it was as unbearable as holding a live wire. When Bessy's mother left, Grace thought of Professor Dzekedzeke's legal aphorism: "If you have neither the law nor the facts, hammer the table!" Grace began to pound the table hard so that her fist hurt, and then suddenly stopped. She stared at all the books in the conference room and thought, pages and pages of laws around me, I can find a way. I always do.

"And what do you expect me to do with wild allegations?" Avaristo spun his pen around his thumb.

Grace had been arguing with Avaristo for the last ten

minutes not to close the case. "I know the police murdered Bessy. I just need more time. You *must* give me more time!"

Avaristo's eyes widened even more. Although he was prone to outbursts himself, Grace knew that he had little tolerance for them from other people. She took a deep breath and spoke again, this time in a calm voice. "The police claim that they released Willbess but he never made it home, and no one has seen or heard from him since."

"Maybe he didn't go home."

"He would've gone home. He had people who loved him! And—" Grace held up the binder in her hands and shook it in the air "—and the police have no paperwork. I've been back twice, and they keep giving me the runaround." She didn't dare mention that she was a wamizimu; Avaristo was already looking at her like she was a lunatic.

"Didn't I tell you to stay away from the police station?"

"How else was I supposed to get copies of the release papers?"

"Grace, listen to me. So far all you have is a theory that when the DPP dropped the charges, the police took it upon themselves to kill this boy because he's a poof."

"What I said was that the police murdered Willbess, and then the DPP, the Attorney General and the Police Chief covered up the murder."

"Oh, thank you, that makes more sense. Seriously, Grace, why would the police murder him? And even if it happened, why would the DPP or the AG ever want to get themselves mixed up in this?"

"I don't know. Not yet."

Grace didn't say that she was out of leads. Big Daddy made her shiver, but what happened with Bwalya since had made her physically sick. After Mrs. Mulenga's last visit, Grace had stalked him at his office and found him at the Inviting Biting Café having drinks with a young lady in jeans and a boob-tube top. She had pulled him aside and tried to appeal to his better instincts: "Bessy's dead and if you don't tell me what you know, you're complicit. What if it was your young brother?" She winced when he said, "My brother isn't a faggot, and if he was, I'd have killed him myself!" He didn't challenge her legal position as Avaristo had, and it wasn't even his vile words or sudden anger, it was his look. Guilty! Bwalya already knew that Bessy was dead. Her whole body turned cold and her saliva tasted so bitter that she had to spit it out. She hadn't intended to spit at Bwalya and they both stared in shock at the bubbles dissolving into the dust next to his shoe. Lawyers used eloquent prose to make their points, not gobs of saliva. She heard the young lady shout, "Who's this crazy bitch?" Reeling, Grace fled the scene.

Now Grace realized that Avaristo was raising his voice at her.

"Sorry, Mr. Daka, what did you say?"

"*Nolle prosequi*, Latin for 'Will no longer prosecute,' meaning the end of the case for us."

Grace shook her head.

Avaristo sighed and continued, "I want you to take a few days off. I mean, look at yourself. And what in God's name did you do to that suit?"

"I washed it." Grace pressed the wrinkles that she couldn't iron out, trying to flatten them with her hands. The dry cleaner had refused to clean it after she had rolled on the ground in it with Mrs. Mulenga, and she didn't have money to buy a new one. At least she had been able to bleach the bloodstains out of the collar of her white shirt.

"Oh, for the love of baby Jesus, I can't have my associates walking around looking like this," Avaristo cried. "Go to Mr. Limbada's Haberdashery and tell him to make you a new suit on my tab. That suit was a dog's dinner even before you destroyed it. Now give me that folder. You've no evidence of any crime; it might be different if you had the body, but you don't, so stop pissing about." He reached out with an open palm.

Grace stood up, stepped out of Avaristo's reach, pulled the folder into her chest and crossed her arms over it. It came to her with startling clarity. "I don't need evidence. I'm going to force *them* to explain what they did to Willbess. I'm filing a habeas corpus petition."

"You're what? Oh no you are not!" Avaristo exclaimed as Grace walked out and took the file with her. "You'll do no such thing and continue to work here! Come back with my file!" Avaristo shouted as she closed the door.

As Grace entered the office the next morning, Mabvuto was leaving with his golf bag slung over one shoulder. "This is his way of saying sorry he closed your case. Don't get mad, get even! Ask Mr. Limbada for the Italian pinstripe.

It's the most expensive." Grace found a note on her desk in Avaristo's heavy penmanship. It read,

Dear Mr. Limbada,
Please attend to the bearer of this note, Grace Zulu, Esq. The urgency of the matter is obvious, as evidenced by the "suit" she is wearing. I'll be eternally grateful if you would outfit my associate in attire befitting our law chambers. All expenses, including a rush order, are to be charged to my account.
Sincerely, AD

Grace fumed all the way to Mr. Limbada's Haberdashery. She wanted to rip up the note and toss the confetti into Avaristo's face. At least that's what she fantasized about as she walked to the north end of Chachacha Road, but she did need a new suit. Esther had given her good directions, and it didn't take long to find the store, "Mr. Limbada's Haberdashery" written in bold, gold lettering on a blue awning. She tried the handle, found the door was locked, then noticed a buzzer. Grace pressed it and within moments a thin, tidy Indian man in a suit and a blue-and-gold-striped bowtie that matched the awning cracked open the door. Grace handed him the note which he read, then opened the door wide with a little bow. "Welcome, Ms. Zulu."

It wasn't like any store that she had been to. It was small but felt opulent, with blue velvet walls and turquoise silk curtains. "Shall we start with fabric?" Mr. Limbada swung open one curtain to reveal several dark rolls fixed to the wall.

"I would like the Italian pinstripe please," Grace said, remembering Mabvuto's advice.

Mr. Limbada looked surprised but said, "Excellent choice." He pulled at a roll of dark blue with faint pinstripes and placed it against her shoulder. Grace stroked the material. It felt thick but silky under her fingers. Mr. Limbada stepped back and nodded. "It suits you well." He rolled the fabric back, returned the curtain and ushered Grace to another curtain, behind which was a three-pane mirror under downlights. Grace turned 360 degrees, twisting her head to see her side and back views. She had a face mirror in her bathroom at Mrs. Njavwa's, and on campus she had had the square mirror built into the cupboard at a height that, standing straight, reflected her torso. Grace had to bend to see her face, or step on a chair to see her storklike legs. From time to time she caught her own reflection in the glass at the office, but had never seen her whole self so clearly. She looked taller, towering over Mr. Limbada, and she had filled out and didn't look quite as skeletal as before. Her eyes looked tired but under the lights her curled hair and skin shone like polished onyx. She moved closer to examine her face in this light. Grace liked how her eyes turned down slightly to meet her high cheekbones, and in this clear reflection, her broad nose, thick lips and big white teeth suited her face perfectly. She touched the cicatrices etched into her cheeks and decided she wouldn't cover them with make-up anymore—they were part of her, they connected her to her ancestors and she had no reason to feel insecure about them. The mirror reflected the beautiful, strong, professional woman she had dreamt of becoming as a village girl. She felt pleased and proud of herself. She stepped back, and her smile dropped as her eyes went down to her suit. She could see every washed-in wrinkle, and the original black was now an uneven dark grey. The fabric had shrunk and left her knobbly knees, thin wrists and part of her forearms exposed, and the hemline was uneven, with a bit of the lining hanging down in the back. Grace knew that her suit looked bad, but the bright lighting made it look so much worse.

"Are you ready for me to take your measurements?" Mr. Limbada didn't wait for an answer. He opened the chest of drawers next to the mirrors and fished out a tape measure which he placed around his neck, a short yellow pencil that went behind his ear and a notepad that he placed on top of the drawers. His movements were quick and efficient. First he held the tape the length of her arms: "Thirty-six inches," he said to himself and wrote the number down on the pad. "Arms up for a second, please." He threaded the tape under her arms and then measured her chest, waist and hips: "Thirty-four, twenty-three, thirty-three. Back straight please." Grace adjusted her slightly stooped posture. "Your jacket will go down to here, and how long do you want your skirt? Below, above or at the knee?"

"At the knee, please."

Mr. Limbada bent down. "Twenty-one inches. Very good."

Yes, Grace thought. This suit is the last item I need to look like the professional lawyer that I am.

Mr. Limbada got onto one knee. "And one final measurement, please step on the tape measure barefoot."

Grace was confused. "You need to measure my feet for a suit?"

"Not a suit, a shoe. A beautiful leather shoe in your exact size."

Grace knew it wasn't his intention, but she felt embarrassed by her dusty, abused kitten heels, which had lost their original shape, the pleather on one heel peeling up like a tiny banana.

"Mr. Daka said a suit. I'm sorry, but I can't afford shoes at the moment."

Still on his knee, Mr. Limbada tapped on her foot to take it out of her shoe. "The shoes are mbasela. They aren't a gift, Ms. Zulu, they're an investment. I did the same for Mr. Daka many, many years ago when he was just starting out and now he's my best customer."

15

DB sat in a wheelchair on his stone veranda. He faced the garden, sunning himself like a lizard with his head tilted up and his eyes half closed. A woolly blanket was draped across his lap despite the heat. He had deteriorated since Grace had last seen him a few months before, when he made a brief appearance at work. His shiny brown skin had turned dull and almost black; his hair had become fine and wispy like a baby's; his lips were cracked and pink; and he had lost a lot of weight. She had heard the rumor at the office from Esther, but one look and Grace knew for sure that DB had AIDS.

Grace remembered when her father was sick, he was either shaking with the chills, or blazing with fever, alternately freezing then boiling to death. She had tried hard, removing then replacing blankets, wiping his body down with a cool rag, adjusting the folded chitenge under his head, but she could never make him comfortable, not even for a moment. Unable to speak, he groaned constantly, even in his sleep, and his body trembled throughout the relentless suffering. Her big strong father reduced to a dried-out husk that shivered and sweated and shed tears out of one eye.

She shook the image out of her head. It was different for DB, money afforded him comfort, and maybe money could buy him time for them to find a cure. For now, at least, he looked comfortable bathing in the sun.

"DB, Grace is here," Mrs. Banda announced cheerfully, as if Grace had been expected. DB opened his eyes completely and smiled. He looked genuinely happy to see her. Grace felt a wave of relief; he was the only one who could save her case *and* her job. She hardly knew DB; she was too junior to interact with him much before he went on sick leave, but when they did talk, she felt that they connected over their mutual love of the law. Even then, she was surprised that the Bandas would be this welcoming. She shook hands with DB and gave a small curtsy of respect, as was the custom in a social setting. His hand felt dry and fragile in hers, as if it would break if she squeezed too hard.

"My dear Muzala, Grace is the brilliant young lawyer I told you about. Top of her class in every subject." Grace's insides warmed at the high praise.

"I have to say how wonderful it is to meet you in person, Grace. DB has not been this excited about an associate since he discovered Avaristo way back when." Mrs. Banda placed a hand on DB's shoulder for a moment. "Drinks, anyone?" Grace didn't want to impose, but before she could decline

Mrs. Banda disappeared through the glass doors into the house, her chitenge caftan floating behind her.

"So good of you to come. Sorry I can't get up just now, a touch of malaria, but help yourself to a chair from over there, and come enjoy the garden with me." He pointed at some folding chairs stacked in a corner of the veranda. Grace carried one over and set herself up next to DB, so that she was also facing the grounds.

"Your garden is very beautiful," Grace said as she took in the manicured lawns, the old trees and the flower beds full of roses, irises, hibiscus and other flowers that she couldn't name. To the right, the water in the pool sparkled. At the end of the garden, Grace could make out a tennis court partially hidden behind a high fence covered with creepers twisting and intertwining along the chain links. Grace couldn't believe that so much land could be a garden.

"I enjoy gardening tremendously. Do you?" DB asked.

Grace thought of her days hoeing, planting, watering, weeding and spreading cow manure across her mother's maize fields. "Not really," she replied.

"You must come back soon when I'm better and I'll show you around and convert you. You can't see it from here, but behind the tennis court I planted an orchard."

"There's more land?" Grace blurted out.

"Oh yes, much more," DB chuckled. "We have guava, pawpaw, mango and lemon trees back there in what I call my enchanted orchard. I also plan to build a small greenhouse for tropical orchids. They need humidity, so I have to figure out some sort of misting machine."

Grace marveled at it all. She hadn't realized that DB was so rich. At the office, he always wore a navy suit, a white shirt and a plain tie, impeccable but never flashy like Avaristo. She didn't begrudge him his wealth, maybe because he had worked longer than she had been on the planet to build his firm, or maybe because it might buy him a stay from his death sentence. Or maybe it was more self-serving; he was the only one who could make sure she kept her job—and she needed her job. She had come so far from sharing a hut with her mother, to sharing a room with Suzanna, to her own en-suite bedroom at Mrs. Njavwa's. But if Avaristo fired her, she wouldn't last very long without an income and could end up in the village and back where she started.

DB was giving Grace far too much information about integrated pest management when Mrs. Banda returned. A man in a white uniform followed her carrying a tray with a teapot, a milk jug, a sugar bowl, a mug, a glass of ice and a bottle of Coke lying on its side. He slowly placed the tray down on the low stone wall that wrapped around the veranda, nodded and melted back into the house.

"Don't let DB get started talking about his flowers," Mrs. Banda warned. Better than pest control, Grace thought to herself.

"We weren't talking about flowers, I'll have you know," DB retorted with a grin.

"Mmm, Grace, did he or did he not mention orchids?" Grace smiled but said nothing.

"I knew it!" Mrs. Banda exclaimed and laughed out loud. Grace wondered how Mrs. Banda could be so jovial at a time like this. She must know he had AIDS, anyone with eyes could see that. It had been rare in the village but it was everywhere in the city. Even so, it was taboo to say "AIDS" out loud, as if to say it would be to tempt fate. Instead, people whispered about "The Long Illness," "The Dreaded," or even "Dead Man Walking" behind hands or behind backs in offices, markets, campuses and even in schools. Grace could now recognize the disease on sight, the darkening of the skin, the wasting, the diminishing of even the biggest, strongest man in the village to skin and bones, to be hurriedly buried under the red earth.

Grace looked but she couldn't see any of the tell-tale signs on Mrs. Banda. In contrast to her husband, she looked the picture of health. Her skin was as smooth as a polished stone, and her jet-black hair was a thick curly mass strangled into a bun. She was plump and seemed to be composed of circles, a moon face with big round eyes, apple cheeks, a snout-like nose and little plump lips, like a doll's. She was no beauty, but she exuded a warmth and confidence that made her attractive. Grace watched Mrs. Banda prepare the tea for her husband. She poured it expertly from the teapot into the mug, chased it with hot milk and a spoon of sugar. She stirred and tasted the tea, sipping it from the spoon and then curled her hand around the outside of the mug to make sure it wasn't too hot before carefully placing it into her husband's own cupped hands.

Mrs. Banda turned to Grace. "I hope Coke is okay, it's all we have." She poured the drink over ice-cubes which crackled and hissed as the glass filled with brown liquid.

"Life now is impossible. There are shortages of everything, even soft drinks!" Mrs. Banda also hissed, as though this was more dire than the shortages of fuel, cooking oil, sugar and toilet paper.

"Thank you." Grace drank down the Coke quickly, gulping and burping softly behind her hand. She noticed both Mr. and Mrs. Banda regarding her and then each other with an amused look. Grace poured the rest of the Coke into her glass and sipped it slowly.

"The only thing my husband loves more than talking about flowers is talking about the law, so I'll leave you to it." Mrs. Banda winked at Grace and floated away.

"Yes, I remember. Pro bono case, a male in a dress charged with Section 155 of the Penal Code: carnal knowledge against the order of nature. The homosexual act alleged to have occurred at a bar called the MacGyver. No named witnesses, and not many other facts on file."

Grace was impressed. She had been told that DB had a photographic memory but she didn't really believe such a thing existed until now. She gave him a summary of the pertinent facts: that Willbess was a juvenile, that he had disappeared while in prison, that she believed that he had been killed by the police in custody, but there was no body. And that she suspected the police, the DPP and the Attorney General were involved in a cover-up. She did not include the gory details of the MacGyver, the visitation from the spirit world, Bwalya or Big Daddy. She self-consciously adjusted her collar so that her scratched neck stayed hidden.

"Proof?" Unlike Avaristo, DB did not accuse her of making wild allegations against the police.

"None."

"Motive?"

"Only a theory."

"What next?"

"Habeas corpus."

"Ahhh!"

"Thoughts?"

"Tricky but not impossible."

"Will you help me?"

"I am always up for a losing battle."

"Avaristo says he'll fire me before he allows me to file this habeas corpus petition."

"Don't worry about that, my name is still on the door."

The next week Grace was back at DB's house to work on the case. Mrs. Banda had opened the front door and led Grace to DB's home office. Before knocking on his door, she had whispered that DB had been feeling unwell and that she could only have one hour with him.

His office felt like a glass box suspended over the garden. It had floor-to-ceiling windows on three sides with a built-in shelf on the back wall crammed with books. DB was sitting in his wheelchair at a long rosewood workbench which ran the length of the front window overlooking a bed of purple and white irises. "Hello, Grace." He looked up briefly and patted a large old leather office chair next to him. The chair was worn, with its leather cracked in places, but it felt comfy when she sat in it. She leaned back, massaged the armrests and couldn't resist swiveling back and forth.

"Our two boys used to love spinning on that thing when they were young, didn't they, DB?" Mrs. Banda said.

"Hmm, yes, darling," DB responded absentmindedly as he organized the books and papers in front of him. Mrs. Banda lifted a small framed photo of a thin young couple with two small boys in school uniform sitting on their laps. Grace barely recognized DB and his wife.

Mrs. Banda laughed heartily. "Yes, believe it or not, that's us and these little guys are our boys, Dennis Junior, and the baby of the family, Manasseh." Mrs. Banda pointed out each boy smiling shyly at the camera. "It seems just yesterday we sent them to boarding school in England, and today they are grown men. Or rather, grown Englishmen who seem to have forgotten their parents, their culture and their home. They don't even want to come visit anymore..."

DB cut her off. "Muzala, please!" He didn't raise his voice, but it had the same effect. Grace wondered what her mother would say about her. She hadn't been home to the village since she moved to Lusaka, over five years ago now. What if her mother fell sick? Would she go? Grace didn't know.

Mrs. Banda put the photo down, picked up a pitcher of water and refreshed her husband's glass, even though it was still almost full. He took a careful sip through a straw.

"Grace, some water, or would you prefer a Coke?"

"I'm fine, thank you. I just had a drink." She didn't want

to trouble Mrs. Banda, who looked exhausted, her whole face seeming to sag. In the short time since Grace had last seen DB, he had lost even more weight, and she noticed that small sores had formed in the corners of his mouth. Mrs. Banda lifted the pitcher in the air before she put it back down on a silver tray next to an empty crystal decanter and two matching glasses. "It's here if you get thirsty." She lingered. "Tea, darling?"

"No thank you, Muzala. Leave us now to do our work."

"Okay, okay, I'm going. Shout if you need anything." Mrs. Banda mouthed to Grace behind DB's back, "One hour," and left the room without closing the door. Grace sensed that Mrs. Banda hovered close by. She understood. She remembered doing the same when her father was dying, hoping that a close vigil could keep death at bay.

DB turned from the pile of books and papers. "Show me the habeas corpus petition." His fingers stretched out like thin black tentacles. Grace handed him the folder and watched him read the papers silently for a long time. Then he picked up a red pen and began to slash and rewrite sections. By the time he handed it back to Grace, she couldn't see her original work for all the red ink. DB was worse than Avaristo!

He must have seen her expression. "Don't worry, it's good. Your reasoning is sound, but keep your prose concise. No puffery. You show how clever you are in court. Here—" He slid some books across the desk to Grace "—study the parts that I've marked for you carefully. Understand them and be ready for any question the judge could possibly ask. Now, very important, we need a strategy for outside the court."

"Outside court?"

"Yes, this isn't a typical habeas corpus petition. Usually the police have the person in custody and we petition to compel them to deliver the prisoner to court. We know that they don't have Willbess anymore, and so what we're really asking the judge is to let us use this procedure to expose murder at the hands of the police."

"There's precedent in the Indian courts," Grace said. "Did you read the Rajan case? They granted a habeas corpus petition where the police killed a university student in their custody."

"Of course, but an Indian case isn't precedent, it's persuasive at best." He coaxed the case out of the stack of papers and gave it to her. Grace saw that he had highlighted areas in yellow and made neat notes in the margins.

"Did you know that before independence, I defended KK against sedition charges?" He didn't wait for an answer. "It was three seasoned barristers flown in from England to what was then Northern Rhodesia to fight one young black lawyer in court for the first time." DB pointed at his chest. "I can still see their red faces when Judge Harrison read out his ruling." He laughed until he coughed, then hacked into a handkerchief for a long time. When his coughing finally subsided, he sucked on his straw a few times and continued. "It was a sweet day indeed, and as much as I received credit for that win, the truth was that it was the protestors outside who convinced Judge Harrison that the colonial era was over. I believe that's what gave him the courage to rule against the Crown."

"That was the sixties and everyone supported KK. It's 1991 now." Grace couldn't believe it was already the end of January, and almost four months since she first met Will-bess. "I just don't think they're going to show up for a gay boy."

"KK wasn't well-known before then, and people didn't show up for him, they showed up for themselves. Look around you, Grace, don't you see? It's the same story, except now it's Zambians oppressing other Zambians and people are sick of it. Power has corrupted my friend KK and he's forgotten what we fought for. And we elites have allowed it by looking the other way."

"I'm not an elite."

"I know, Grace, and I thank you for opening my eyes again before it's too late."

"I don't understand what this has to do with our case."

"Everything! When the police kill children with impu-nity, they are saying that the rule of law is dead. We need people, lots of people, to say enough! To remind them that the people hold the power and we won't allow this any-more."

"How do you plan to organize this?"

"Me? You mean how do *we* plan to organize this. We'll do it the same way we did it back in the sixties." DB's eyes shone and he looked energized. "We ask all of our friends to come out."

Grace thought about her friends: Suzanna, Mrs. Njavwa,

Father Sebastian and Mr. Patel. She could count them on one hand, with a finger to spare.

"I've only got four friends," she confessed.

DB nodded. "I find that hard to believe, but not to worry, I've lots of friends and I plan to call every one of them. But you're not off the hook, we need young people too, so you must bring your four friends, and tell them to bring their four friends, and so on and so forth."

Grace didn't have the heart to tell DB that three out of her four friends were septuagenarians.

"It'll be like the good old days, we'll organize a mass protest like nobody's business. Mark my words, Grace, they won't get away with killing young Willbess."

16

Grace heard rustling behind the door and so kept on banging. Eventually Suzanna emerged. "It's you? *Bwanji!*" she greeted Grace and retreated back into the dorm room, leaving the door open. Grace hadn't seen her old roommate since yanking her out of the MacGyver Bar. She stepped over a mess of empty bottles and plastic cups, some with a bit of pale liquid in them, others with cigarette butts and a few with both. What a pigsty, Grace thought. Even for Suzanna this was bad and she felt glad to be done cleaning up after her.

"You just getting up? It's afternoon, you know." Grace kicked away some clothes on the floor to clear a spot where she could stand. She watched Suzanna search through a pile heaped at the end of her bed, sniff a shirt and reject it, and then pull her purple dungarees on over her bra. She then began to search for something on the floor.

"Don't just stand there, help find my ciggies. There should be half a pack somewhere."

Grace lifted an empty packet off the floor and flipped it upside down to show Suzanna that it was empty.

"Fucking parasites couldn't even leave me one," Suzanna complained. She fished a half-smoked cigarette out of a cup, straightened it out carefully and lit it. She sucked on it desperately, then exhaled with satisfaction and grabbed a Mosi from under her bed. "Ha! Those parasites didn't find you, my little darling." Suzanna kissed the bottle, then curled her lips around the cigarette again and took another drag. Watching her smoke someone else's old cigarette left Grace queasy. Overwhelmed by the smell of stale beer and cigarettes, she stepped outside onto the balcony and pushed the doors wide open to air out the room. Suzanna followed her out.

"Nice suit."

"Thanks. It's tailor-made. For once I have something that fits me." Grace stuck her arms out to show Suzanna. Mr. Limbada had delivered the suit and shoes to the office himself. The suit had its own bag, and each shoe came wrapped in soft turquoise tissue inside a blue box with a gold ribbon. Grace admired the bows on the front of her new kitten heels. "My boss got it for me. I'm paraphrasing but he said I was an embarrassment to the firm in my old one. Called it a dog's dinner." Grace laughed, it seemed funnier now.

"He bought you a suit? Why? Are you bonking him?"

"What? No! Of course not. He's my boss and he's old."

"I slept with an old man once. My dad's friend. I had such high expectations but it was disappointing. His penis was so small I found it hiding behind a pube." Suzanna began to bray with laughter. "Worst five minutes of my life!"

Grace had to laugh too. Four years of living together meant that Grace could no longer be shocked by Suzanna's sexual exploits or her proclivity for lurid details.

"So, you're still a virgin then?"

Grace shrugged. She wanted to be able to laugh at herself like Suzanna and tell her about fumbling around in a Fiat 127 with Bwalya, but his betrayal still felt too raw and painful. Besides, Suzanna had a big mouth. It was one thing for her to share her own secrets with glee and embellishment, but she was also indiscreet about Grace's. She remembered Suzanna had told the Londoners that Grace's mother had sold her for twenty kwacha, as if it was some big joke. When Grace stormed out of the room, she heard them laugh even harder. Worse still, when she confronted Suzanna later, she was dismissed. "We were only joking. Friends tease each other about everything, nothing's sacred. That's the point! Birdie makes fun of my whore-bag father; calls him Ball-sac instead of Balzac, but you don't see me getting all huffy-pops about his stupid name. You're going to have to stop being so sensitive if you want to be one of the gang." But Grace did not want to be one of the gang.

"Are you listening to me?" Suzanna asked, bringing Grace back to the present. "I said, you need to lose your virginity. It's an albatross around your neck."

"What's an albatross?"

Suzanna kept the cigarette clenched between her teeth and puffs of smoke came out of her mouth as she said, "Not sure, but I know that you don't want it around your neck. Here, make yourself useful and open this for me." Suzanna handed Grace the beer, wanting her to open it with her teeth, as she often did when they couldn't find an opener.

"Come on, Suzanna, you're not going to start drinking again this early."

"*Come on, Suzanna,*" she replied, mimicking Grace's accent. "First you say it's too late, and now you say it's too early. And hair of the dog doesn't count."

Grace took the bottle but didn't open it. She got to the point of her visit. "Are you still social secretary of the student politburo?"

"Of course. And now without you here as official party pooper, it gets wild. They should make me president for life, baby!" Suzanna began to dance and yell the refrain of a popular rap song: "'*Your motherfucking father says to do what's right, your motherfucking mother says come home tonight, I say burn the motherfucker down and dance to the light!*'"

Students glared up at them from the quadrangle below, where they sat on the grass in ones and twos hunched over their books. It was study week, and one lifted her finger to her lips, signaling for Suzanna to be quiet. She responded with her middle finger.

Grace shook her head and sighed deeply. "I need you to pay attention, this is serious." She explained to Suzanna that she needed her help organizing a student demonstration outside the courthouse during the hearing. "They killed

Bessy—" Grace choked up "—and we need to show them
that we won't take it anymore!"

"I almost got expelled for the riots last year, and while I,
your fearless heroine, was staring down the neo-colonialists
and neo-fascists on the frontlines, you were cowering in
the library. And now you want me to stick my neck back
out and incite *another* riot for you? Hell no!"

Grace had refused to participate in the "Dog Food Riots"
on principle; she was grateful to eat free food in the cafeteria
and found that it tasted just fine. For reasons Suzanna could
never explain, instead of protesting peacefully, the students
burned the chancellor's car and rolled it into the lake. From
the library window, Grace had seen the riot police swarm
in and Suzanna and the other ringleaders driven away in
Black Marias. Grace had taken a taxi she couldn't afford to
Suzanna's parents to tell them about the arrest. Her father
had gotten the charges dropped and bought the chancellor
a new car, so Suzanna was allowed back to university after
a few weeks, but the others were expelled.

"I'm not talking about rioting. I'm talking about a peaceful student demonstration off campus for justice and human
rights."

"Are you going to open my beer for me or not?"

Grace was getting annoyed. "No, I'm not."

Suzanna tried to take the bottle, but Grace held it up
over her head and out of Suzanna's reach.

"Stop being a bitch. If you're not going to open it for
me, give it back!" Suzanna jumped and tried to snatch the
beer but instead knocked it out of Grace's hand. It smashed

against the concrete floor, sending shards of brown glass, white foam and gold liquid across the balcony. They both jumped back.

"Fuck! You just broke my last bottle, you better go and buy me another one right now!"

"You should be studying instead of drinking."

"You're going to walk to the shebeen across Great East Road, dig into the pockets of that new suit and replace the beer that you smashed."

"I didn't smash it, you knocked it out of my hand."

"You broke it and for once in your life, you're going to pay me back. No more pleading poverty."

"If you keep drinking instead of studying, you'll fail again. If it wasn't for all your partying you would've graduated with me last year. I've been meaning to talk to you about it—Father Sebastian says that you can attend the youth AA meetings at St Ignatius Church on Friday nights."

"Father Sebastian? You don't get to talk about me with that fat fuck."

"Come on, Suzanna, there's no need for such foul language. I'll go to the meetings with you, I think they'll help."

"Who the hell do you think you are? If it wasn't for me, you'd still be that stinking villager who walked in here five years ago! I'm the one who taught you how to talk, to dress, to even spray your fucking armpits. I bought you food and clothes. If it wasn't for me, you'd've been back in that village of yours long ago. You think a job and that stupid suit suddenly makes you better than me? Go fuck yourself!"

Grace felt as though she had been punched in the stomach. She had always excused Suzanna's vitriol as alcohol talking, but this time Suzanna was sober and it couldn't be explained away or justified. Grace stepped over the foam and shards of brown glass and made for the door. Before she left she turned to Suzanna. "Since we're counting favors, I did your school work, cleaned up your drunken messes, carried you out of parties and saved you from your alcoholic self too many times to count. So let's call it even."

"Saved me?" Suzanna laughed hysterically. "That's a good one. Take your messiah complex and shove it up your ass!" She flicked her lit cigarette at Grace. "That's right, *voetsek*!"

Grace marched through the eucalyptus forest at the back end of the campus, rerunning the fight in her mind. Suzanna's cigarette hadn't even hit her, but the lit, grubby stub flicked in her direction offended Grace the most. She wished that she had thought of something equally devastating. Walking through the shanty town, she tried to calm herself down. She remembered her father's words, "No one can humiliate you without you accepting it." Like basic contract law, Grace thought, offer and acceptance, take your emotions out of this. Easier said than done. She could still taste the bile in her mouth.

A taxi almost hit Grace as she absentmindedly stepped into Kalingalinga Road. She stopped to gather herself before attempting to cross the busy street again. Suzanna was definitely not worth getting killed over. Grace took the shortcut through the abandoned airfield that separated the shanty town from the rich areas of the city. Walking across this barren no-man's-land, she thought about their early days on campus. It was true that Suzanna had bought Grace almost all of the clothes she wore and gave her luxuries like cocoa butter and Impulse deodorant, but Grace had never asked her for any of it. She had always believed that Suzanna was generous, but now she re-examined the meaning. Was it still generosity if it wasn't hard-earned money? Suzanna's father gave her lots of money whether she was good or bad, passed or failed, or heaved the chancellor's car into the lake. And all those clothes Suzanna had given her were mostly things she had declared ugly before tossing them at Grace—"My mother's taste is hid-eee-ous!" By the time Grace reached Saddam Hussein Boulevard, she concluded that their friendship was nothing more than a mutually convenient relationship, and this fight a wind that had blown away the topsoil and exposed its shallow root system.

17

Grace and Mrs. Njavwa had finished dinner but lingered at the dining table. Grace had eaten several lumps of nshima and lumanda with her one piece of grilled chicken leg. The portions of beef, goat, chicken and fish Mrs. Njavwa served were getting smaller and smaller as prices soared, but Grace felt grateful that, regardless of the cost, Mrs. Njavwa still insisted on at least one portion of protein to go along with generous servings of nshima and vegetables. Grace devoured the crispy skin of the chicken and all the tender flesh and then picked up the bone again to chew off its soft ends and suck out the marrow. Mrs. Njavwa snatched the bone from Grace's mouth and gave it to Davey, who crunched and swallowed before Grace had time to protest.

"Bones are for dogs, not nice young ladies. Now, where was I?"

"You were saying something about the UNIP Women's League," Grace replied.

"Oh, yes, do you know what the Women's League did to protest during the independence struggle?" Mrs. Njavwa didn't wait for Grace to answer. "We stripped and used our naked breasts to shame the colonialists. It was powerful, I tell you." She raised her fist in the air.

"Are you suggesting that this nice young lady go bare-breasted to the courthouse?" Grace began to giggle as she tried to picture the two of them standing with their fists in the air and their breasts hanging down like pawpaw. "As a lawyer, you know I'd have to keep my court wig on." They both burst into uncharacteristically raucous laughter.

"Forget that student union, why not try the real one, the Zambia Congress of Trade Unions?" Mrs. Njavwa asked.

"Everyone knows that the unions are banned and its leaders are in hiding."

"You should talk to Diana's boy, Freddy Chiluba. He's the one to help you."

"Freddy? You mean *Frederick* Chiluba?" Grace had read about him in the papers. He was the leader of the trade union and the government had recently issued a warrant for his arrest. "You're in touch with the opposition? I thought you were a staunch UNIPist," she said, referring to President Kaunda's ruling party.

"I was a UNIP freedom fighter, which is different—and besides, wrong is wrong. Killing a boy is wrong, no matter what!"

"The newspaper said Frederick Chiluba is also in hiding, so how would I go about finding him? I wouldn't even know where to start."

"I've known Freddy since he was in nappies. His mother was my neighbor on the Copperbelt for years. Leave it to me."

The old man driving the taxi ignored Grace's attempts at conversation. He had remained silent from the time he'd picked her up. Mrs. Njavwa greeted him warmly through the passenger window of the battered vehicle as Grace got into the back seat, but she made no introductions. She wondered how they knew each other. Perhaps he had been a freedom fighter with Mrs. Njavwa. The man put one hand over his heart as a sign of respect, but didn't cut off the engine, and stepped on the accelerator as soon as Grace closed the car door.

He drove like a taxi driver, fast, with an elbow hanging out of the window, but Grace was sure that he wasn't one. With a shock of white hair, he seemed too old, his pose too studied and he did not look relaxed. Besides, he had a suit jacket and tie neatly folded on the passenger seat next to him. No taxi driver she'd ever met wore a suit to work. The old man drove up Independence Avenue, whipped around the downtown circle twice, checking his rear-view mirror, before catapulting onto the Kafue Road without signaling. Grace put her seatbelt on.

"Do you know Mr. Chiluba?" Grace tried again. She was hoping for some useful background information that might help her convince Frederick Chiluba to help her. She had grilled Mrs. Njavwa about him, but apart from the fact that he was a staunch Christian, she mostly shared stories of when he was a naughty boy. Grace knew almost nothing about the man leading the trade union, or organizing political opposition against KK, and despite her efforts to engage him, the old man drove on without responding. As they left the Lusaka city limits, Grace asked, "How far are we going?" Instead of answering, he pulled in his elbow, rolled up the window almost to the top and plunged a cassette into the player with his thumb. Smokey Haangala's voice filled the car. His falsetto grated Grace's nerves; she was already on edge about meeting Chiluba, and she was worried about the case. It would be easy for a court to dismiss Willbess as poor and unimportant; nobody in the system seemed to care except Grace, who cared too much.

At least that's what Avaristo said. According to him, she had lost all professional objectivity. He was still furious with her for going to DB to force the habeas corpus petition. "Scurrying to DB behind my back, making this mess of yours even worse!"

Even without Avaristo's insinuation, she was haunted by the thought that maybe, if she'd handled things better with Officer Lungu, Bessy would still be alive. She thought about him during the day, and dreamt about him at night. She had a recurring dream that she and Bessy were fish, swimming in the Nyakawise. Unlike the real river, the water was clear and, as only happens in dreams, she knew exactly where she was, and was unperturbed about being a fish. She darted around the rocks, and Bessy chased her.

When a shadow fell over them, they looked up and could see a cat's claws hanging over the side of a rock, just above the surface of the water. She swam closer and the paws became boots, and Grace realized that Bessy was no longer behind her, he was being yanked out of the water by a large hook in his mouth. In an instant, both Bessy and the boots disappeared and all that was left of him was a thin red trail of blood. The blood began to spread quickly until the whole river turned thick and red, and Grace couldn't breathe anymore and she'd wake up gasping for air.

Grace needed to focus, to think through what to say to Frederick Chiluba. She couldn't concentrate with Smokey's high-pitched warbling, so when the old man slowed down at a bad patch of potholes, Grace snapped open her seatbelt, stretched between the seats and ejected the cassette. "Hope you don't mind," she said after the fact. The old man looked at her in surprise, as if he had just realized that there was someone else in his car.

About ten minutes later, he finally spoke. "We're almost there." His voice came in a hoarse whisper. He looked hard into his rear-view mirror before suddenly pulling off the tarmac. The old man revved his taxi up a gravel road to the top of a hill and parked next to a small stone monument that seemed to have been erected in the middle of nowhere.

He told Grace to wait and got out, walked down the road and looked around before beckoning to her. She could see his mouth moving but the sound was caught and carried off by the wind. He pointed and then moved towards a path cut through the high grass. Grace got out of the car

and followed him as he threaded his way up and then down
the surrounding hills. The old man was surprisingly swift
and agile and Grace struggled to keep up. It would've been
nice if someone had mentioned that they would be hiking
hills and not riding an elevator into an office building, she
thought. She would not have worn full lawyer regalia—
her new pinstriped blue suit from Mr. Lambada's Haberdashery and her polished-to-a-shine kitten heels. Grace
slid on some small pebbles and only just managed to save
herself from going down. She cursed her shoes. The old
man paused briefly at the skidding sound, then continued
downhill. Grace discovered that she could move a bit faster
if she walked sideways like a crab.

   She finally caught up with him at the bottom of a hill,
where he waited next to lines of barbed wire that fenced
off a coffee plantation. The old man held down a wire and
ducked through the gap, careful of his little white Afro,
and then held two wires apart for Grace. She hesitated before hitching up her skirt and clambering through, trying
not to flash the old man. Once through, she turned away
from him, smoothed her skirt back down and cursed again
under her breath. They walked in silence, side by side,
through neat rows of dark green bushes. Grace could see
the clusters of small fruit had started to turn from green to
red. In a matter of weeks this plantation would be team-
ing with pickers, their burlap sacks slung over thin hips or
small backs and their nimble fingers plucking at ripe red
berries from dawn to dusk. Grace hated the harvest. When
she was young, it meant being pulled out of school to twist

maize cobs off their stalks, or to heave cassava tubers out of the ground. Even worse was when their crops failed and she was hired out to other fields for a pittance that went to her mother. When she was older and refused to leave class, harvest meant battling both her mother and hunger. "If you want to eat, you work. If you want to study, you better get full on your books," her mother had said and meant it. Grace massaged her hands. Just being near these ripening berries made them feel stiff. She felt grateful to work in an office and would take a year of Avaristo over one day back in the fields.

They found Chiluba sitting under a lone msolo tree in the middle of a row of coffee bushes. He sat in overalls on a goatskin stool with another empty stool facing him. He stood up and embraced the old man, who stooped low to hug him. They patted each other on the back for a long time.

Frederick Chiluba was not what Grace expected. She had never seen a photo of him but reading about him, she had subconsciously developed a picture in her mind. She couldn't describe exactly what she'd thought he'd look like, but this diminutive man with a tiny hand sticking out waiting to shake hers, was not at all how she imagined the great leader of the Trade Unions. Everything about him was miniature. He could not be more than five feet tall or weigh more than sixty kilograms. His narrow face was crowned by a scruffy afro, and the scraggly whiskers hanging from his cheeks and chin were that of a young man trying to coax a first beard. But his hair was starting to recede and he had grey wisps at his temples. He had risen through the ranks to become leader of the unions, so Grace figured that he must be old—at least forty.

"Mulishani." He placed his small paw of a hand in Grace's. His grip was strong and vicelike, and he pumped her hand vigorously.

"I'm fine, thank you," she replied in English and curtsied slightly.

"Walishimba icibemba?" Chiluba asked.

"No, I don't speak Bemba. I speak Nsenga, English and a bit of German. I'm also teaching myself Latin." She wanted to impress him, but realized that she sounded pretentious and wanted to kick herself.

"Latin? I commend you, comrade. I dropped out of school young—actually I was thrown out, but that didn't stop me. I educated myself too. Ba Mayo Njavwa encouraged me and gave me books to read, although I'm not sure romance novels were the best thing for a young boy." He chuckled, exposing his slightly discolored and ragged teeth. "Sorry about the precautions. I hope you weren't too inconvenienced. My comrades believe it's necessary for my safety." He pointed to the coffee bushes, and Grace realized that there were more people around them. "They're afraid that you might be a UNIP spy. You see, the UNIPists want me to disappear off the face of the earth, but we can't let fear hold us back, can we, Comrade Grace?" He stroked his whiskers as he talked. She was surprised that he knew her name. He motioned for her to sit and so Grace arranged herself with some difficulty on the low stool, tucking her long legs awkwardly to the side. Frederick Chiluba sat back down on his stool, stretched out his legs and crossed them at the ankle. His feet, in flip-flops, looked neat with mani-cured toenails. Not the feet of a laborer.

"Ba Mayo Njavwa tells me that you can help me. That you have a case that could be the catalyst I need to move the MMD beyond the unions."

Grace was surprised that Mrs. Njavwa had reversed the roles of who needed whom.

"Have you heard of the MMD?" he asked.

"Not really. I heard that there's an opposition party but I don't know much about it."

"We're not a party, we're a movement pushing for change, for KK and UNIP to step aside. MMD stands for Movement for Multiparty Democracy. And we need Young Turks like you to join us. Will you?"

He seemed to expect an immediate answer so Grace nodded.

"Good!" He smiled and clapped his little hands. "Now tell me about the case. Ba Mayo was quite vague."

Grace tried to present the case from a legal point of view, focusing on the presumption of innocence, the burden of proof, the suspected murder and the habeas corpus petition. She brushed over the Penal Code, and the alleged crime of homosexuality. Frederick Chiluba squinted his button eyes as he listened. He stopped her every few minutes to ask questions, and she noticed him constantly scanning the blue hills around them.

"How old was the boy?"

"He was seventeen at the time. He'd have just turned eighteen last month; his birthday was on Valentine's Day."

"My son Castro is almost the same age." He shook his head. "What was an underage boy doing at a disco?"

"He was an entertainer, a very talented dancer," Grace said, banishing the image of Willbess taking clients into that awful little room at the MacGyver. It was shady under the msolo tree, and a cool breeze was blowing through the farm, but sweat poured down Grace's back.

"Why would they single him out to accuse him of such a heinous crime?"

Mrs. Njavwa had mentioned more than once that Frederick Chiluba was a born-again Christian, and Grace understood that to mean that he was probably homophobic. She swallowed hard, she wanted water badly. "They had no case against him, the DPP filed a *nolle prosequi*, that's when—"

Frederick Chiluba cut her off. "I know what it is. I've had my share of legal problems. But I'm troubled, Grace, very troubled by the unbiblical nature of the crime."

She thought about the first and last time she saw Bessy in prison, his swollen face and how he had looked at her in hope. "The only thing unbiblical is the police killing a defenseless boy."

"You seem like a smart young woman and I'd like to help, but we need a high-profile case that is less, shall we say, controversial. I'm sorry but this one isn't right for us." Chiluba looked past her and resumed scanning the hills.

"Mr. Chiluba—" She raised her voice so that he would look back at her "—controversy, if you want to call it that, serves your cause. One could argue that challenging the UNIP one-party state is controversial, and putting yourself forward as a presidential candidate is controversial, so why would you worry about controversy now? Aside from being an important legal issue, this is a matter of public interest and something that people will talk about."

"But not in a good way. Most regard these people as abominations."

"And you?"

"I agree. Of course."

Of course! The words landed like a slap from her mother. A small strike that ignited an anger that spread through her like molten lava. Grace knew that she had to control her emotions, keep the sharp edge out of her words, stay calm and steer Frederick Chiluba towards something that he could relate to. "How can you talk about a movement if you won't fight for basic human rights?" she said. "How do you expect young people to support you, if you won't support us?" Her voice shook a little but she hoped he couldn't tell how angry she felt. As Mrs. Njavwa had cautioned, anger was rarely a useful emotion.

Frederick Chiluba continued to avoid her gaze. "No. No! I'm afraid—"

Grace knew it was over. Nothing she could say would move him. The lava inside her erupted and she cut him off: "Yah, yah, so much for not letting fear hold us back." Grace struggled to get up from the stool and the old man materialized from behind the bushes and helped her. She shrugged him off and resisted the urge to kick the stool.

She'd wasted a whole day coming out to the middle of no-where to talk to this homophobic coward.

"Ba shi Castro," the old man intervened, "she has a point. What are we fighting for if we turn our back on this boy?" Grace realized that there must be something wrong with his vocal chords as his voice didn't go higher than a whis-per, and he seemed to struggle to get out more than a few words at a time.

"Muna, what happens if I put my reputation on the line, and this boy pitches up alive and well?"

"He won't, Ba shi Castro. I'm a grown man and prison almost killed me." He rubbed his larynx and Grace noticed a thin scar across his neck. "We have only six months before the next election, something needs to happen very soon."

"This hearing is already on the court calendar for 11 April," Grace added, shifting closer to the old man. Maybe all wasn't lost.

"You're from DB's outfit, right?" Muna asked Grace, who nodded. "Freddy, Dennis Banda represented KK in the fifties and sixties before independence. It'll be a power-ful statement if we have DB on our side. Grace, is DB first chair on this case?" She could see his vocal chords strain-ing. Grace realized from his language that Muna must be a lawyer too, or must have been at one time.

"DB is on the court record as first chair," Grace re-sponded, not untruthfully. She knew that DB's illness was getting even worse, but he could still get better.

"He was a true freedom fighter back then," Muna added,

smiling at Frederick. It was the first time since he had picked her up that she saw him smile.

"He still is," Grace corrected.

Muna pulled Frederick to his feet. "Comrade Freddy, this is the opportunity we have been waiting for. Imagine the headlines," he whispered, hoarse and excited: "'KK's Lawyer Joins Opposition Fighting Corrupt Government!'" He raised his free hand up in the air with his index finger and thumb out, and wagged it in some sort of hand signal.

Frederick caught his hand and shook his head vigorously. "No, Muna, no! I won't have my good name associated with a homosexual." He said the word slowly, enunciating every syllable, ho–mo–sex–shol. "I've made up my mind. We'll find another case."

The car hissed when Muna turned the ignition, and after a few clicks, died. What next, Grace thought, locusts? Boils? Frogs? She knew nothing about cars so she waited by the stone monument while the old man popped the hood of the car and disappeared under it. She noticed a small metal plaque had been hammered into the stone:

THE MUNALI PASS

TRADITION STATES THAT IT WAS FROM

THE SUMMIT OF THE HILL ON THE WEST

OF THE ROAD THAT DR. DAVID LIVINGSTONE

OBTAINED HIS FIRST VIEW

OF THE KAFUE RIVER ON 14TH DECEMBER, 1855.

HE CROSSED THESE HILLS

DURING HIS GREAT TRANS-AFRICA JOURNEY
FROM ANGOLA TO MOZAMBIQUE
AND THE PASS IS NAMED AFTER HIM, MUNALI
(THE RED ONE).

Grace wondered if Dr Livingstone was a redhead, or if they just called him that because of his reddened skin. She thought about how Father Sebastian's pate became distressed within minutes of being in the sun. She couldn't imagine a white man trekking across the continent with such delicate and revealing skin. Grace examined the backs of her hands. Her skin was a dark shield that revealed nothing of the roiling emotions she felt inside. She wondered if Livingstone knew how far he still had to go to reach Mozambique. Did he look down at that torpid snake of a river below and feel dejected? Had he also wanted to quit, but like her, found himself too far in?

Muna slammed closed the hood of the car. "It's the battery," he whispered. "We're going to have to push-start it."

Grace threw her jacket and shoes in the back seat, and rolled up the sleeves of her shirt. "You get in and drive. I'm strong enough. I'll push."

18

Grace sat on a reed mat on the floor, facing the window, her legs stretched out in front of her, going over the opening statement again and again in her mind, while Mrs. Njavwa, sitting on a chair behind her, parted lines in her hair, scratched out dandruff with an afro pick and rubbed her scalp with a foul-smelling yellow pomade extracted from a jar at her feet. Grace was going to be alone in court. DB had been admitted to UTH, University Teaching Hospital, and Avaristo had refused to go with her. "Career suicide with a side of financial ruin? No thank you!" Mrs. Njavwa tugged gently at Grace's hair, moving her head this way and that as she wove thin cornrows down to the nape of her neck. Grace hadn't slept well for the last week but with Mrs. Njavwa's hands on her, she felt soothed and began to doze and dream.

She lifted her arms, as she had done when she was a toddler, and her father lifted her up and swung her onto his back in a single movement. He covered her with a chitenge, pulled one end over his shoulder, the other under his arm, and heaved her into place. He tied the extra material into a tight knot over his heart so that Grace was secure on his back. The women of the village clucked and scolded, "It's women's work to carry children!"

"She's too big! Look at those long, dangly legs!" But her father waved them off with a laugh and kept walking. In her protective cocoon under the chitenge, Grace rested her head against his back and listened to her father humming the freedom song "Tiyende Pamodzi" to the beat of his heart. They walked along the Nyakawise glowing copper in the sun, and watched a flock of black birds fly so close to the river that their wings appeared to touch the waves.

"There," Mrs. Njavwa declared, lifting Grace's head off her thigh. Grace woke up feeling happy. Usually dreams of her father meant reliving his pain and suffering, and she woke up with tears in her eyes.

"Look! How beautiful!" Mrs. Njavwa handed her the mirror. Grace looked at her reflection carefully and smiled. She did look beautiful. She liked the contrast of her inky black skin and mulberry gums against her big white teeth. Even her slightly droopy eyes didn't look sad or tired. She held the mirror up higher and turned from side to side to admire the neat, narrow cornrows with their tails twisted into a stylish bun at her nape. Mrs. Njavwa showed her a hairpin made of shiny rhinestones before using it to secure the bun. "This was a gift from my late husband, David. I remember he'd help me place it so my hairdo looked just

right; back then my hair was lovely and thick like yours."
Grace felt her bun tighten as Mrs. Njavwa inserted the pin.
"David claimed it brought good luck, and I think it did. I
want you to have it. And no arguments please, save them
all for tomorrow." Grace felt a rush of love towards the old
woman in the mirror, peering over her shoulder.

The next morning, Grace directed the dilapidated taxi
off Saddam Hussein Boulevard and down the unnamed dirt
road lined with flame trees that led to the back entrance
of the High Court. The taxi driver deposited her and her
box of folders, books, legal pads and pens at a tall iron gate
and then reversed into a three-point turn and sped back up
the lane in a whirr of dust and fallen flowers. Grace could
hear a commotion but couldn't see what was happening
behind the ten-foot wall around the courthouse. A security
guard appeared, peering at her through the narrow space
between the wall and the iron gate.

"Identity card." He stuck his hand out through the space.

What would she be doing in black robe, bands and horsehair wig pinned firmly to her cornrows if she wasn't a lawyer going into court? She felt annoyed but didn't want to
get into an argument with the security guard and risk being
late. With the box on one knee and struggling to maintain
her balance in her heels, Grace fished her card out of her
robe pocket and placed it on the guard's open palm. He
inspected it, handed it back and then opened the gate just
wide enough for her and her box, even though there was

no one else behind her. He shut the gate, keeping his eyes trained to the right.

Even before she got through the gate, Grace saw that a wall of policemen in full riot gear had formed a perimeter across the main entrance of the courthouse. From what she could see, it looked like a big crowd was in front of them. Someone began to chant into a megaphone. She stopped to listen, her long neck craning and her court gown billowing behind her like dark wings. "*Abash* Fascism!... *Abash* President Kaunda!... Free Willbess!" People cheered and clapped.

Grace watched a young man climb up the Lady Justice statue in the High Court's yard and wave a sign that read "Habass Corpass!" in red, dripping paint. Who were all these people? Where did they come from?

Inside, the court chamber was window-less and sound-proof, so Grace could no longer see or hear what was happening outside. Despite the early morning, the court-room was already hot and sour. She was surprised that the gallery was full. She saw Willbess's parents and sisters squashed together somberly in the front row between Leo Kanta, the famous newscaster, and a local politician whom Grace recognized but couldn't name. They were all focused on a woman in a pink pant-suit and a matching hat fighting with the row behind her to keep her hat on. They all went quiet when Grace approached. The Mulengas took turns hugging her: Loveness, the twins together, Mr. Mulenga and last Mrs. Mulenga. She embraced Mrs. Mulenga far longer than appropriate in a court-room, drawing in an energy she felt the older woman bestow on her.

Grace moved to the front of the court-room and stood in the middle, unsure at which of the two desks she should sit. Did the petitioner sit on a particular side, or was it first come first serve?

"No surprises, the bloody air conditioner is broken."

Avaristo appeared to materialize out of nowhere. He wrinkled his nose at the stale air, threw his briefcase on top of her box, lifted it all out of her arms, and led the way to the desk to the left of the judge's bench.

"Mr. Daka! You're here!" Grace felt a big wave of relief. "I didn't expect you. I thought you were against the whole thing!"

"Believe you me, Grace, I am. I most certainly am. For the record, I came under duress. DB made me come." He placed the box and his briefcase on the desk, and then wiped his head with a handkerchief, even though he didn't appear to be sweating.

"How is he?" Grace asked.

Avaristo shook his head. "But he's a stubborn old man, he'll bounce back." He sounded upbeat, but his wide eyes watered and his voice cracked at the last word. Avaristo coughed several times to cover it up. Grace began to tear up too. DB should be here, he should be first chair on this case, not me, she thought as she unloaded her box. She placed a big folder on the table, careful not to disturb her detailed notes, then extracted a dog-eared Penal Code, a book on habeas corpus case law and finally several pens and two writing pads. Avaristo lifted the last item in the box, her father's Bible.

"What's this then? Hoping for divine intervention?"

Grace snatched her Bible, placed it back in the box and put it on the floor so that it was touching her feet. She felt better with it near her. More confident. "Despite your sarcasm, I think God is on our side. Did you see those crowds outside? I can't explain it, except to say it's a miracle."

Avaristo scoffed. "If kwachas are miracles then, yes, I suppose you could call it that."

"What do you mean?"

Avaristo covered his mouth and whispered, "DB made a very big donation to Frederick Chiluba. He's underwriting the MMD on condition that they support this case. Naturally, I advised against it."

Grace's stomach turned. "I thought for a minute that people genuinely cared about Bessy."

"Maybe they do, maybe they don't, what matters is that they are out there and their presence sends a message to the judge, the police, and even to the President."

Before Grace could ask more questions, the Attorney General barged into the court-room with three lawyers and two legal assistants, each carrying a cardboard box. They followed him around like ducklings as he made his way around the room, greeting various people. He stopped at their table, shook hands with Avaristo, but ignored Grace.

"Avaristo Daka, Esquire, in a court-room litigating," the AG said. "Well, well, well, this must be a first."

"It's been a while, but it's not my first."

"A horrible case for your big comeback. I've known you to be many things, but not a fool."

"From the crowds outside, I'd call it a big case, and let's let the judge be the judge. Precisely the point of litigation, wouldn't you say, old chap?"

"You mean that circus outside? When they hear the full facts, you'll lose in the court of public opinion too, if that's your strategy."

"My only strategy is justice." Avaristo gave the Attorney General his *I wish you death* grin and turned his back on him, pretending to look through Grace's folder.

"Arrogant prick," Avaristo muttered as the AG walked away. "Give him five minutes and he's boasting about his days at Oxford. Well, *I* went to Oxford, *he* went to Oxford Polytechnic!"

"What's the difference?" Grace suppressed a smile.

Grace watched the minute hand of the wall clock jerk a full circle. She fidgeted, cracked her knuckles, then gave in to the impulse and gnawed her fingernails down to nubs. She hadn't chewed on her nails since primary school, where the headmaster and his ruler cured her of the habit. Eventually the heat killed her nervousness but it was too late for her nails. Grace looked back at the gallery. Everyone was fanning themselves except the woman in pink who had fallen asleep with her hat still on. Grace's horsehair wig felt murderous. She considered taking out the pins and removing it for some relief, or lifting one side to fan underneath, but she was worried that the judge would walk in.

She envied Avaristo, who had his wig off; its neat curls and tail looked like a small white animal sleeping in his lap.

"Whose idea was black robes and horsehair wigs in the tropics?" Grace asked, breaking the silence between them.

"Someone who hates lawyers."

They both laughed a bit too hard, relieving the tension.

After another thirty minutes of suffering, the bailiff finally walked in. "All rise!" he announced in a baritone. They all stood. Avaristo quickly placed his wig back, lining up his hands to his ears to make sure that it wasn't askew.

Judge Simbyakulya entered with a full-bottom wig enveloping his round face, white bands around his thick neck and a red robe sweeping majestically behind him. He nodded at no one in particular and sat down heavily. The room erupted momentarily with wails as people jostled for space on the tightly packed gallery benches. The court fell quiet again when the judge opened his file. He looked around the court-room, and his gaze seemed to settle on Avaristo but a lazy eye made it difficult to be sure. The judge cleared his throat.

"Counsel for the petitioner, please begin."

The judge's eyes widened and he cocked his head slightly when Grace stood up, her chair scraping the parquet floor. "Grace Zulu, Esquire, my lord." Out of the corner of her eye she saw the Attorney General and his team exchanging looks, then grins. Grace stood quietly for a long moment, smoothing her robe and adjusting the strangling white bands that lawyers had to wear in court. She rubbed her ndembo; she felt physically uncomfortable, but mentally clear, and surprised by how calm she was.

"Habeas corpus in legal Latin means 'You have the body.'" Grace turned to the Attorney General sitting to her right and stared at him. She straightened her back and stood tall, and projected her voice so that it carried strong and sonorous across the court-room. "*You* have the body."

"Objection, my lawd, I clearly do not."

"My lord, it is just a literal translation from Latin," Grace responded.

"Overruled. Carry on," the judge said without looking up from his scribbling.

"Our petition today is simple: we ask you to compel the Attorney General to bring Willbess Mulenga to this august court. His inordinately long imprisonment without court mention is *prima facie* illegal, and his fundamental right to freedom abrogated. He has not been seen by his family or his friends for seven months and I, his counsel, have been illegally denied access to him."

The gallery murmured its disapproval.

"Willbess Mulenga's right to liberty is enshrined in our constitution, but our constitutional rights are not self-executing, and so our courts must enforce them. Without enforcement, our Bill of Rights is reduced to meaningless, empty words written on paper rendered less useful than toilet paper."

A man in the gallery laughed, and others shushed him.

"Ms. Zulu, are you playing to the gallery in my court?"

"No, my lord."

She had argued with DB, who insisted on adding "toilet

paper" to her brief. It had been their last meeting before he went into hospital. He had looked frail but his voice was strong and his eyes shone. He explained that she needed to speak to all people through the press in the gallery, and convinced her to keep the language in for the newspapers.

"Today we petition that the court sends a message to the executive that we will not allow our rights to be trampled on by the boots of the police."

"Amen!" shouted the man who had laughed.

"Bailiff, remove that person from my court!" Judge Simbyakulya bellowed. Grace paused as the man, protesting loudly, was escorted out by the bailiff. She understood why Judge Simbyakulya's nickname was "Judge No-Nonsense."

When the door was closed again, she continued, "The writ of habeas corpus is one of the most important protections of liberty under the law. By granting this petition, the court can compel the police to either bring the prisoner to the court, or tell the court the terrible truth about what they have done to this young man."

"Objection!"

"On what ground?"

"Her statement is prejudicial."

"How so, counsel? Overruled."

Grace continued, "To refuse this petition today is to refute the spirit and purpose of habeas corpus law, and to undermine the rule of law and the very foundations of justice." Grace sat down. Avaristo nodded and gave her a terse smile.

The Attorney General stood and, with one hand in his pocket, began pacing back and forth in front of the court-room as he spoke. "My lord, I must applaud junior counsel's effort to rewrite the rules of habeas corpus. A particularly laudable effort, given that she has just been called to the bar, when, last year?" He paused for an objection but Avaristo placed his hand firmly on Grace's elbow.

"As much as I admire Miss... Miss—" He looked back at his table, and his second chair started flipping through his notes. The Attorney General looked annoyed but continued, "As much as I admire young counsel's boldness, I do have to wonder if the client is best served by a novice when Mr. Daka is present and—"

"Ms. Zulu's been called to the bar, has she not?" The judge sounded impatient. "You'd do well to get on with your own arguments, counsel."

"Much obliged, m'lawd." The Attorney General cleared his throat before continuing, "The writ of habeas corpus is an ancient prerogative writ, harkening back to the 1200s. Under this writ, there must be two elements: an order of detention that is wrongful; and a person in custody. It is a procedural writ that cannot be used as a fishing expedition in the case of a missing person. For the court to set such a precedent would be to open the floodgates for every missing person in the country." The Attorney General turned to the gallery with his arms open as though he expected applause, and then turned back to the judge. "Habeas corpus law is well established and can only be rewritten by an act of Parliament, not ambitious young lady lawyers. Perhaps counsel can be forgiven as too young to know what's in the law books. The missing person in question is known to be of dubious character, frequently found at the Mac-Gyver Bar a den of iniquity. He was arrested for unnatural homosexual acts, crimes under the laws of Zambia and the laws of God."

He waited for Grace to object. Avaristo held her arm again but DB had already cautioned her to avoid the trap of arguing the crime: "An accused homosexual will find no friends in the court, so let the AG say what he's going to say, and you stay focused on the habeas corpus petition."

The Attorney General hesitated but then continued, "Willbess Mulenga was released by the police and ran away, too ashamed of his crimes to return to his God-fearing family. He is probably having a good time as we stand here wasting the court's time and resources. For all we know, he could be frolicking away—"

The judge interrupted, "Do you have anything more to say on the writ, counsel?"

"Yes, my lord. I apologize but the nature of this crime upsets me so. I beg the court's indulgence and forgiveness." The judge waved his pen in the air like a conductor for the Attorney General to continue. "This is a missing person case, and what the petitioner is seeking is an inappropriate extension of habeas corpus law. If the court awards this petition, it will set a terrible precedent. We therefore humbly submit to this honorable court that the petition is dismissed as improper, and an abuse of the court system."

Grace stood. "As the Attorney General has stated himself, habeas corpus is a procedural writ, and it's well established in law that procedure is *always* open to a court's interpretation, provided it is not expressly prohibited. There is no such prohibitive rule here. Perhaps the Attorney General is too old to remember what's in the law books." The gallery laughed, and the Attorney General glared at Grace. She held his gaze.

"Approach the bench." The judge's eye drifted so Grace wasn't sure if he was looking at her, but she came forward anyway and stood under the judge, who was scowling from his seat. "Both of you!" Judge Simbyakulya barked, and the Attorney General scurried forward. "The decision today is a serious one, and will be made by this court based on the law. Playing to the gallery will not serve you in my court."

"Yes, my lord," they both answered, heads hanging like naughty children.

Grace returned to her desk, and looked at Avaristo, who winked. She resumed when she had regained her composure. She had to finish strong.

"It is the court's duty to protect citizens from illegal detention. This is a core function of the court, and there is no reason to shy away from exercising its jurisdiction here. Indeed, to do so would set the dangerous precedent of the police sidestepping the law by simply denying that they had a prisoner in custody. My lord, this is not a case of a missing person. Willbess Mulenga was detained; this fact is not denied, and is corroborated by affidavits from his family who witnessed his arrest, and I myself who saw him in custody. Since that one time I saw him, when he and I were both manhandled by the police, neither his family, friends nor

I have seen him again. He disappeared, or rather, he was disappeared by the police."

"Objection! An unsubstantiated and false allegation."

"My lord, we have affidavits from the family."

The Attorney General replied, cutting his eyes at Grace, "My lord, these affidavits cannot speak to what happened after the petitioner was released from custody."

The judge nodded. "Duly noted and sustained. Please move on, Ms. Zulu."

"The police claim that they released Willbess, and that he must have run away, but they have no release documentation, as required by the law, and have no explanation as to why no one, not his loving family, not his extended family, not a single friend, schoolmate or neighbor ever saw him again. If he is a missing person, as the Attorney General keeps asserting, then he is missing at the hands of the police."

"My lord!" The Attorney General jumped to his feet.

"Objection sustained. Counsel, I won't tell you again to refrain from making unsubstantiated allegations."

"Thank you, my lord!" The Attorney General raised his arms to the ceiling and flapped them once, like a little bat.

"Sit down, counsel. Not you, Ms. Zulu."

Grace jumped up again. "In closing, my lord, granting this Great Writ compels the executive to do the right thing, the morally and legally correct thing, and have the police either deliver Willbess Mulenga to this court, or explain why they cannot do so. They must explain what they have done to him. Your decision today will send one of two messages: that the police can detain any of us with impunity and no regard for our rights, or that our rights, guaranteed by the highest law in the land, will be protected by the courts." Turning to the Attorney General, Grace closed as she had opened: "Habeas corpus in Latin means 'You have the body.' Do the right thing and give Willbess Mulenga's body back to his family to bury him."

"This is preposterous! I move that you find her in contempt."

"Attorney General, do you have anything further to add in response to this petition?" As soon as he shook his head no, Judge Simbyakulya stood. "Thank you; I will render my decision within the week. This court is adjourned."

"Bloody hell!" Avaristo surveyed the crowds that seemed to have multiplied while they were inside. From the top of the stairway in front of the courthouse, the crowds had indeed spilled out of the court's yard and spread as far as Grace could see. Someone had put a pair of purple sunglasses on the Lady Justice statue.

The crowd was uncharacteristically quiet. Grace couldn't see him but could hear Frederick Chiluba's sonorous voice and the words "father," "son" and then "Amen." It sounded as though he had been leading the crowd in prayer. Then the crowd began chanting, "Justice! Justice! Justice for Willbess!" Grace smiled at Avaristo. Frederick Chiluba may have been motivated by DB's donation, but the crowds wanted justice for Bessy.

The sound of shattering glass rose above the chanting.

Grace saw the policemen pull down their visors and raise their shields and long batons. The atmosphere instantly changed, and the crowds began to jeer and taunt the police.

"Neo-fascists! Neo-Nazis! Neo-colonial dogs!" shouted the voice on the megaphone.

"Oh my God," Grace whispered, "it's Suzanna." Who else would add "neo" to everything? Who else would put purple sunglasses on Lady Justice? The policemen moved forward in lockstep. Grace craned her neck and frantically scanned the thousands of faces for Suzanna, Mrs. Njavwa and Father Sebastian, but couldn't find any of them. She hoped that they had left. Then she heard Frederick Chiluba's voice again clearly on the megaphone.

"We are here to *peacefully* protest the police snatching our young brother Willbess Mulenga from his father's house. The police took him but they never brought him back." The crowd murmured in rising anger. "Minamate, minamate! Please stay calm! We are here to demand justice for Willbess! We are here to demand that the courts hold the police accountable! We are here to demand human rights and democracy are restored to our beloved Zambia!" A cheer went up. Grace looked to the police and was relieved that they didn't move.

19

Avaristo and Grace found Esther waiting for them in the courthouse parking lot. She told them that DB's situation had worsened and Mrs. Banda wanted Avaristo at the hospital immediately. Avaristo looked panicked. "Come with?" he asked Grace. They jumped into his Peugeot and he sped to the hospital, where he parked diagonally, taking up two spaces next to a tire-less ambulance on bricks. They started towards the building, but then Avaristo suddenly ran back to the car. She watched him take their court gowns and wigs from the back seat, and lock them in the trunk.

"Who would steal these relics?" Grace asked him when he caught back up with her.

"Each of those relics cost 500 pounds sterling. I'm not taking any chances."

UTH was a labyrinth of concrete corridors and cloisters. Avaristo asked a couple of nurses in pale blue uniforms and white caps for the VIP ward. They pointed to another corridor. Avaristo and Grace cut across a quad where dozens of people were taking respite from the wards. Some stood in clusters talking; others sat on chitenges with babies crawling about their laps; a man with one leg leaned on his crutches while his empty pant leg flapped in the wind; a skeletal woman was being transported in a wheelbarrow by a young man who had tears running down his cheeks; and children chased each other, shrieking and laughing. Grace envied these small children, oblivious to the misery and death around them. So many died here that the hospital's nickname was "The Departure Lounge." This is the most depressing place in the world, she thought, feeling overwhelmed.

"Pee-yew!" Avaristo snatched his silk handkerchief from his jacket pocket and smothered his face. Grace also stuck her nose into her blouse. She recognized the unique, acrid smell of decomposing human flesh. "It's the morgue," she said from her armpit. It wasn't a smell you forgot. The year that floods unburied the bodies in the village cemetery, the stench hung in the air for days after her father and a few other men had reburied them. When far enough away, Grace sniffed the air like a meerkat and signaled to Avaristo that it was safe.

"Ugh! Disgusting! I hate coming to this place," he said.

They followed a sign with a big red arrow that read "VIPs—3rd Floor." A horse-faced nurse at the reception desk tried to tell them that visiting hours were over, but Avaristo strode passed her without stopping. Grace heard the nurse protest but followed closely behind Avaristo without looking back.

They found Mrs. Banda at the end of the ward, sitting on a small bench outside a closed door. She stood up when she saw Avaristo and hugged him. She looked a far cry from the elegant woman who had regally swept through her mansion a few weeks earlier. She wore a shapeless cardigan over a t-shirt and a chitenge wrapped around her waist. Grace could tell that she had lost weight; her fat cheeks seemed to have collapsed into jowls, and she had dark rings around her eyes. She stepped between Grace and the nurse who had caught up with them, and spoke to her with authority. "Sister, they're not leaving, but they won't stay long." The nurse hesitated but nodded, and went back to her station.

"How is he?" Avaristo looked at the closed door like it was a portal to hell.

Mrs. Banda shook her head. "He's stopped talking and eating. They're feeding him through a tube right now. I can't stand watching it. Any luck with the boys?"

"I got them first-class tickets from London, but they're still refusing to come."

"See if you can't convince Junior, he's less stubborn than Manasseh. I don't understand why they can't forgive their dad. I'm the only one with the right to be angry, not them. He's worked so hard for them, sacrificed so much for them, and this is how they repay him!" By the end of the sentence, her voice was at a high pitch. Grace felt awkward, standing in the middle of a private conversation. Mabvuto had told her that DB's sons were angry and ashamed that their father had contracted AIDS, and so far Avaristo's efforts to cajole, bribe and threaten them with disinheritance weren't working. Grace looked away, scanning the ward for the horse-faced nurse, who had disappeared from her station.

"I know he's waiting for them. He's hanging on for his boys."

"They'll come. They'll be here very soon," Avaristo promised.

Another nurse emerged from DB's room and informed Mrs. Banda that they had finished feeding him, and that he had kept it down. Through the open door, Grace could see DB propped up by pillows behind his head and both sides of the hospital bed. He was just skin draped over bones— even his skull appeared shrunken. His eyes were half open, but he didn't blink and didn't seem to register his surroundings. Grace followed Mrs. Banda in but Avaristo froze at the door. Mrs. Banda stood on one side of the bed and took DB's hand, while Grace sat on a chair on the other side. DB looked like her father just before he died, except for all the tubes that seemed to sprout from everywhere, the medicine bags dripping colorless fluids into both of his arms, and the bleeping heart monitor. Death warmed up, she thought, looking at him. She put her hand on top of his, and it was cold to the touch. Not even death warmed up, just death. Grace placed his hand in between hers. The room was quiet except for the bleeping sound. Avaristo fled.

"Tell DB how the case is going." Mrs. Banda broke the silence. "Tell him all the details," she urged. "I know he wants to hear everything..." Her voice caught. Grace wanted to cry too but remembered that when she was down, Suzanna could always cheer her up with absurd stories and she wouldn't give up until she had Grace laughing.

Grace told DB about the protestor's sign that read "Habass Corpass," about Judge Simbyakulya's cockeye, and how she and the Attorney General weren't sure who he was looking at and lambasting. She told him about her septuagenarian landlady who had wanted to protest topless, and how her best friend, Suzanna, had put purple sunglasses on the Lady Justice statue. Grace knew that she wasn't as funny as Suzanna, but she did manage to make Mrs. Banda laugh.

"Lady Justice still had the shades on when we left," Avaristo added. Grace hadn't heard him come back. She could tell from his expression that Avaristo had never seen dying before. Death was one thing, but the undignified, painful, leaky, smelly, leeching process of dying altogether another. Avaristo stood next to Grace and she handed him DB's hand. He held it carefully as though handling an egg.

"You were right, old chap, I needn't have worried," Avaristo said to DB. "Grace was marvelous in court today. Simply marvelous."

Grace was shocked to hear such praise from Avaristo. DB's eyes seemed to focus for a second before he closed them. They all stared at the heart monitor, and Grace could feel her own heart beating wildly in its cage. To their collective relief, the green line continued to leap across the small screen, announcing with every beep that, contrary to appearances, DB was still alive.

20

"All rise."

Grace watched Judge Simbyakulya intently, looking for a clue as to which way he would rule, but his face remained impassive. He didn't look at her, or the Attorney General, his phalanx of lawyers, or the gallery whispering behind them. The judge's cockeye didn't wander, and both eyes remained fixed on his bench as he walked unhurried and then rearranged his robe to sit down. He waved his hand for them all to be seated. When everyone was settled and quiet, he pulled out a piece of paper and cleared his throat. Grace tried her best to look as calm as Avaristo sitting next to her. She too folded one hand over the other and placed them on the desk, resisting the urge to rub her pounding temples, or chew the nubs where her fingernails used to be.

"This is a habeas corpus petition in a case where the detention of Willbess Mulenga has not been disputed, but counsels for the petitioner and for the respondent have presented two opposing views of what happened. On the one side, counsel for the petitioner has argued that Mr. Mulenga was never released, and is thus petitioning this court to force the state to either produce Willbess Mulenga, or explain what happened to him in their custody. She has gone so far as to allege that the police have 'disappeared' her client."

Something in the judge's tone quashed Grace's optimism.

"On the other side, the Attorney General has explained that although the petitioner was indeed in police custody, he was released as required by the law after the Director of Public Prosecutions issued a *nolle prosequi*. Willbess Mulenga's release papers, however, were conveniently misplaced by the police. The Attorney General has gone so far as to offer his own theory for why Willbess Mulenga ran away, which I dismiss as speculative and conjecture."

Grace's quick sideways glance at Avaristo caught a fleeting smirk.

"After due consideration of the arguments, I find that neither side has presented sufficient evidence to support their version of events. Regardless of whose story I personally find more credible and compelling, my decision is based only on corroborated evidence and the long-established habeas corpus law."

On hearing this, Grace slumped in her seat. Judge Simbyakulya continued reading without looking up.

"I recognize that an extension of these laws has been

accepted in India, but that is not the case elsewhere in the Commonwealth, and not the case here in Zambia. As much as I have sincere sympathy for the Mulenga family, our habeas corpus jurisprudence is clear. Accordingly, the petition is hereby denied. There will be no order as to costs."

Judge Simbyakulya rose and left the court.

Grace looked back at the Mulenga family in the gallery. She could tell from the confusion that they were still deciphering what the judge had said. Then the gallery erupted in angry noises, and Grace heard Mrs. Mulenga cry out, "Bessy!" She was almost carried out of the court-room by Mr. Mulenga and their three daughters, and the gallery followed with their heads bowed low as if in a funeral procession.

"I hate that bastard," Avaristo muttered under his breath, sending a murderous look at the Attorney General, who was slapping the backs of his team as they left the court-room.

Grace pinched her nose and held back her tears. "Me too," she replied, but she hated herself more for failing Bessy and his family. She had convinced herself that they would win. Could she have said more to persuade the judge to be courageous? Or was she expecting too much of him to rule against the government that appointed him?

"I was very impressed with you, Grace."

"We lost." Grace unpinned her wig. She felt like flinging it across the court-room. She scratched her scalp. Avaristo took his wig off as well, looked around to make sure the court was empty and then extracted his handkerchief from his suit and rubbed his head with vigor. Grace imagined it must've been even itchier for him without any hair.

"Grace, you convinced the gallery, and I suspect you convinced the judge that the police killed that poor boy." He gave his brow a final wipe and then placed the handkerchief in his trouser pocket. "Jolly well done."

"Jolly well done? I'll tell that to Mrs. Mulenga." She knew she was pushing it with Avaristo, but she didn't care.

"Even if we had won, Grace, do you really believe that the police would hand over a dead body?"

"They would have to, wouldn't they?"

"Let me tell you what happened in that Indian case you cited after the court granted the habeas corpus petition—absolutely nothing! To this day the family doesn't know what happened to their son's body. Why? Because a dead body means a crime, a crime means an investigation, and the government doesn't want an investigation. This trial was about exposing an atrocity, and you did that."

Grace was thinking about the Mulenga family, and how their pain and anger had become her own. "It's not enough."

"We're lawyers and like it or not, this shitty court system is where we dwell."

"We need to appeal."

"No, Grace, this is where it ends. The firm is already on its knees, and we've just been officially blacklisted from government business. Do you understand what that means?"

"We have private clients."

"In this country there's no such thing as a private client. Every agency, every company, every organization is directly or indirectly government controlled. Our clients are already moving to other firms."

"So Bessy's dead, and we give up and go home with our tails between our legs?"

"No, Grace, I go groveling to those government prats to lift the ban so that I can continue to support my family and my clueless associates."

"Gandhi never gave up and ultimately he won even bigger battles."

"Ultimately it ended very badly for Gandhi, and if you stay on this path, it will end badly for us too."

Grace shook her head. "He brought an end to British rule in India, and we can bring this government down too!"

Avaristo looked around in a panic. "Jesus Christ, Grace, don't ever say that out loud again. It's treason. And by the way, you are not bloody Gandhi!"

"How can I face the Mulengas? And what about all those people out there protesting? I have to keep going otherwise Bessy would've died for nothing. I understand if you have to fire me."

Avaristo sighed. He looked exhausted. "We'll all be in the unemployment line soon enough. Give me your stuff and go on then." He helped her fill the box and put his briefcase and the two wigs on top. Just before Grace left the court-room, Avaristo called her back. "Your wig! Put it back on."

"No, not the wig!"

"Yes, the wig! People need to see it and know on sight that you're Bessy's lawyer."

He helped Grace hold the horsehair wig straight while she pinned it back in place.

21

When Grace emerged from the court-house, the crowd outside erupted in applause. Don't they know that I lost the case? she thought. But the protestors continued to pat her on the back and they propelled her to the front of the crowd, where she was reunited with the Mulenga family, along with Father Sebastian and Mrs. Njavwa. To her surprise, Mrs. Mulenga gave her a long hug. In Mrs. Mulenga's arms, the tension in her body eased and some of the pain of losing subsided. She wanted to stay there longer when Frederick Chiluba awkwardly joined the hug while someone took a picture. Then he got busy organizing Grace, the Mulengas, Father Sebastian and Mrs. Njavwa into a line. He positioned himself between the two statuesque women and laced his arms into theirs, shouting instructions to the others to do the same. They then marched up Independence Avenue with their arms interlinked, waves of protestors behind them all singing "Tiyende Pamodzi" as loud as they could. It felt spontaneous but Grace wondered if DB had orchestrated it. She imagined him giving Frederick Chiluba a typed memo with notes in the margins in his tight, neat handwriting. *Sing the freedom song. Everyone knows it's the President's favorite, and it will send an unequivocal message to all with ears.*

Suddenly what sounded like fireworks went off behind them. Everyone stopped singing and looked around, confused. Towards the rear of the crowd, Grace could see batons and tear gas in the air. Within seconds, people were screaming and running in every direction. Frederick Chiluba was spirited away by a man on a motorbike, the Mulengas sprinted off in one direction and Grace followed Father Sebastian and Mrs. Njavwa in the other. She tried her best to shield them from running people and hurried them along, flapping like a great bird protecting her slow-moving chicks. Father Sebastian led them off the main road and down a dirt path to a side gate of the Seventh-day Adventist church. Grace heaved with her shoulder until the latch gave, and the three of them and a few more protestors tumbled in. Father Sebastian banged on the church doors. The pastor must have been watching the protests from the church because the doors were flung open immediately. They dove in and hid behind the pews as the pastor closed and locked the doors behind them.

Grace feared the police would storm the church and she, along with the others, would be yanked out of their hiding places and arrested. She thought about Bessy, and shook at the thought of going to prison. It wasn't long before the commotion and shouting outside subsided and, aside for an occasional siren, it became eerily quiet. After about half an hour on the floor, Mrs. Njavwa heaved herself onto a church pew and rubbed her knees. Within a few minutes, everyone else moved to the pews too. The pastor stayed at his post behind the window curtain keeping vigil. All the light in the church had faded to black before he declared it safe to leave. He dispatched the other protestors, and then drove Father Sebastian, Mrs. Njavwa and Grace home in his pick-up, using back streets even though the whole city seemed deserted.

On the way home, the pastor harangued Father Sebastian for allowing dark forces to lure him into legal battles and political protests. He glanced at Grace in her gown and wig every time he said "dark forces," but Grace was too tired to defend herself. Father Sebastian didn't argue either. He even agreed with everything the pastor said—"Yes, a foolish thing for a man of the cloth... Indeed, far too old... As always, you are quite right, my brother"—but Grace could tell that Father Sebastian was pleased with himself. The pastor could also tell and by the time he dropped her and Mrs. Njavwa off at their gate, he was becoming heated and kept repeating the same reprimand. He reminded Grace of the village priest who didn't realize that, after a certain point, a scoldee would close their ears like a crocodile submerging into the river and hear no more.

It felt like the longest day in her life when Grace finally reached her room. She sat on the end of her bed and felt around her head, pulling out all the pins that secured her wig. Once off, she tossed it towards the dresser near her bed but it missed. Avaristo would be apoplectic if he saw his expensive wig on the floor, but Grace was too exhausted to pick it up. She kicked off her shoes, lay her head on her pillow and immediately fell asleep on top of the covers with everything else still on.

Grace sat at Mabvuto's desk and read the article he had pointed out to her in the national paper: "Disbar Dis-Grace!" In it, she was described as the devil's lawyer, promoting homosexuality and turning Lusaka into Sodom and Gomorrah. Grace checked the newspaper from cover to cover, but there was no mention of the anti-government protests at all, only fetching pictures of KK waving his white handkerchief visiting a spruced-up wing of UTH. Grace didn't recognize it as the same UTH that she had just visited.

"The police fired tear gas and were beating people up. We've no idea how many people got hurt, or arrested, or if anyone was killed. It's like the protests didn't happen at all," Grace said to Mabvuto, who was tapping golf balls down the lane between their desks. He paused and without looking up from his putter said, "When the *Times of Zambia* ran an article about the miners protesting on the Copperbelt, the editor was fired. Oh, and remember last year when that idiot Lieutenant Luchembe got drunk, took over the government radio station and played reggae until the police dragged him out? *Everyone* at the station got fired for their involvement in the so-called coup. Controlling the media is Repressive Regime 101."

Grace nodded. She shouldn't have been surprised; it was a government-owned newspaper, all the news outlets were. "And this picture of me looks like a mugshot." She had never seen the photo before but remembered it being taken during her registration at university, her first few days in Lusaka. The photographer had asked her to smile and she, indignant at the suggestion, had refused. In the village, a photo was a serious event where everyone dressed in their Sunday best, stood still and looked at the camera with a sober expression. Eventually Grace learned that in Lusaka, one was supposed to look happy in photos, and Grace would shout "Cheese!" along with everyone else when a camera was pointed in her direction. In this picture, her eyes looked wary and uncertain, and her hair was cropped close to her skull. She remembered using a razorblade on her head because the boys in school seemed to bother her less the more she looked like a boy. She recognized the collar of the shirt as the old school uniform that she'd worn until Suzanna gave her new clothes and tossed her old ones over the balcony. Grace touched the neat bun of her hair, and then ran her fingers down the fine fabric of her new suit. It was her in this photo, of course, but she found the image disconcerting, like a snake happening upon its old, dead skin.

Putter still in hand, Mabvuto returned to his desk to re-examine the grainy black-and-white photo. "Fresh off the bus, as the saying goes. Bald, wide-eyed, but not wholly unattractive if you're into that village-beauty look."

Grace ignored him. She read the article again. "Do you think they can have me disbarred?"

"The Law Association only considers complaints from clients, and according to this article—" Mabvuto tapped the newspaper "—your client is the devil, so I think you're okay." Mabvuto laughed until he started hiccupping.

"It's not funny. This is my life!"

"Should have thought about that before you decided to piss off the government, Dis-Grace." Mabvuto placed his putter back into his golf bag, but left half a dozen golf balls under their window. Grace took over the lane to pace. It was one thing to be fired by Avaristo, but another to lose her license. She'd be done as a lawyer and wouldn't know how else she could make a living in Lusaka. Just thinking about having to go back to the village made Grace feel physically sick.

"Stop worrying, Grace, we lawyers are like the South African Boers. We fight like cats and dogs amongst ourselves, but if anyone attacks us from the outside, we form a laager to protect our own."

"Even if it's the government?"

"Especially if it's the government. They can push everyone else around, but not us. Besides, I'm on the ethics committee. Avaristo has me sit in as his proxy and I've got your back. No one's taking away your license."

Grace felt better. Mabvuto was right, the Law Association was one of the few spaces the government didn't control and they couldn't simply revoke her license. Relieved, Grace sat down again.

Mabvuto jumped onto his chair, took a moment to balance himself, and then puffed out his chest. "I'm your Boer! De Klerk to your Nelson Mandela! If they try to stitch you up, I shall set you free!" It had taken some time, but Mabvuto's humor was growing on her.

Grace tried her best to mimic Mandela's South African accent and deliberate way of speaking. "Meneer de Klerk, just wait until I become president! You'll have to answer for the twenty-seven years I spent in prison."

Mabvuto's Afrikaner accent was more successful. "Ma boy Nelson, jest because I let you out of prisin, doesn't mean I'm going to let you have ma office. Setting you free just bought us another hundred years of apartheid."

"The writing's on the wall for apartheid."

Mabvuto abandoned mimicry and said, "No, man. The Whites are too scared of what'll happen to them if the Blacks get power. That's the reason no one wants to leave power. Not in this lifetime anyway. Not de Klerk and, despite your efforts, not KK either."

Just then Esther's head appeared in the doorway. "Your uncle's here," she said to Grace. "I've put him in the conference room," and she disappeared again just as quickly. Grace didn't have any uncles. Could it be Mr. Patel? She hurried to the conference room but froze when she saw Big Daddy sitting at the long ebony table that ran down the center of the room.

"If you don't leave right now, I'm going to get security."

"Lawyer Grace, I'm sorry about last time. I wanted to frighten you and make sure you stayed away. I don't like people coming to my place uninvited."

"I don't like it either."

"I have information for you." He rolled his seat back, eased off a shoe and began to rub his foot. "Oh, it's really paining me. Gout," he explained, as if Grace had asked. "I should have worn a flip-flop but it would look awkward with my nice suit, eh?"

"What information?" Grace was interested, but she stayed standing in the door-frame. She knew that Big Daddy was fast, violent and crafty and she couldn't let her guard down for one second. He might not even have gout, maybe he was just trying to disarm her. Grace tried to remain calm and willed her heartbeat to slow down. Few people physically frightened her, but Big Daddy did.

"Sit down, I don't like people standing above me."

Grace ignored him. "What information?"

"I know who killed Bessy. A police officer named Muntu. He told his superiors that Bessy died accidentally during his interrogation, but that he wasn't sorry because it meant one less homo on the planet." Big Daddy shook his head and laughed bitterly. "He should've killed himself if that was the case. Munali is a muthanyula, as they call us. I'm told that he got married and disappeared from the scene for a while, but then he resurfaced at my club the night of the fight. I don't know how, but Bessy and Munali knew each other. I saw Bessy walk up to him as soon as Munali walked in and they started to quarrel. They went outside for a while, and when they came back in, Munali punched him."

"I'm confused, Munali or Muntu?"

"Same person. His real name is Muntu but his street name is Munali because of his red hair."

Grace remembered Munali was Bessy's yellow dog's curious name, and then an image of the officer with red hair at the police station flashed in her mind. Did she meet Bessy's killer? Grace felt light-headed and braced herself against the door-frame. "Is he mixed-race, red hair with green eyes, working at Lusaka Central Police Station?"

"Could be the one. He stands out. Handsome but very arrogant chap. Thinks he can walk in and destroy my club? I didn't know who he was and it took me a while to find him, but I would've beaten him up anyway, minister's son or not." Big Daddy slashed both hands in Grace's direction, like a wild cat. She took another step back.

"Mr. Muntu, as in the Minister of Justice?"

Big Daddy nodded. The cover-up by the Attorney General, the DPP and the Police Chief now made sense to Grace. "Who told you about Munali?"

Big Daddy eased his shoe back on, stood up and stepped on it gingerly. "A policeman who used to collect money from the MacGyver. He said he felt bad about what happened, seeing as he was supposed to keep the police away. I think he felt worse about not having that extra cash, now that the MacGyver's closed. He told me about Munali, and then he asked me for money. How stupid is this man?"

"Would he be willing to testify?"

"He's stupid, but not that stupid. No policeman will testify against another, especially not against Munali. He's a dangerous man from a very powerful family."

"I can't do anything with this information. Hearsay is useless to me."

"Eh, eh? Lawyer Grace, information is never useless."

22

"Do you know how long it takes for a body to decompose?" Grace asked Father Sebastian as he poured tea and hot condensed milk into two mugs. He handed one to Grace and began sawing at a fruitcake covered in icing.

"I'm not— What's the English word for *ein Pathologe*?" he responded, still sawing until the whole cake was sliced.

"A pathologist."

"Thank you. I'm not a pathologist." He balanced two large pieces carefully on a small plate and placed it on the desk in front of Grace. His old hands strangely resembled the cake—pale, flaky and covered with dark splotches. "My sister sent this stollen all the way from Germany." Grace ate the slices of cake quickly in big bites and licked the icing off her fingers. Father Sebastian put a third piece on her plate. "Why are you asking?"

"It's been eight months since Bessy disappeared and I'm

worried that it'll soon be impossible to identify his body. They say the rolling protests are putting pressure on KK and he's actually considering multiparty elections. Someone must know something and I believe that if there's a new government, they'll feel safe to come forward."

"I heard the rumors too but who's to say that KK wouldn't win a multiparty election?"

"The protestors say so. If the election is free and fair, he won't win. I just hope it won't be too late to find Bessy. I feel like we can't have closure without finding him."

"We?"

"The family, me, the country!"

Father Sebastian picked up his cake and nibbled. "From the little I know, decomposition depends a lot on the weather. In Germany during the war, we preserved bodies in the snow in winter until it thawed enough to dig graves. Here in Zambia, we need to put people in the ground quickly, otherwise they start to stink."

"I was at UTH last week to visit my boss, Mr. Banda, and the smell from the morgue was overpowering. You could smell it from a mile away." Grace snorted as though the stench was still in her nostrils.

"The electricity at the hospital has been on the fritz for months. The morgue fridges go on and go off, so of course the place stinks to high heaven. With so many dying of AIDS the bodies are piling up. I heard that Mr. Banda has AIDS too."

Grace was surprised that Father Sebastian knew about DB. Though it was a big city, the elite were a small group who gossiped relentlessly—but who would gossip about DB with a priest? A lifetime of achievements reduced to four letters, said with malice, no doubt by someone unworthy of speaking his name. Grace wished that DB could return to the office in robust health in his impeccable blue suit and shut the gossips up.

"Will you ask God to spare Mr. Banda's life? I think it may have more weight coming from you."

"We shouldn't fear death, Grace. It's inevitable and as Catholics we should look forward to an eternal life with our heavenly Father."

Grace didn't fear death, she feared dying. DB was suffering, and his wife and everyone who loved him suffered along with him. And Grace worried about his soul. How would God judge him? What measure of good deeds outweighed the bad? Did professional accomplishments count in God's court? She didn't know much about DB's personal life beyond his illness. She surmised from the conversation at the hospital that his sons were angry with him for cheating and contracting AIDS, and he could have passed it on to his wife and maybe others. How would God assess such a fatal mistake? And he was rich; the Bible said it was easier for a camel to go through the eye of a needle than a rich person to enter the kingdom of God. She thought about her own father, who had made the same mistake, but he was poor. Was there really a different standard for the poor? Grace found the Bible confusing. In some places it sounded hard to get into heaven, and in other places easy and straightforward. God was sometimes a loving and forgiving father, and other times arbitrary and capricious.

"Let's pray to our heavenly Father that when his time comes, Mr. Banda is ready and able to enter the gates of heaven." Father Sebastian knelt down to pray. Grace moved slowly to the parquet floor and hoped that he would be quick. But the priest bowed his head and prayed in Latin for a long time. Grace only understood a few words, "*domine…omnipotens…portas…lucis et pacis,*" but she listened to the cadence of the priest's words. It had been a long time since Grace had found comfort in prayer, or believed that God was listening, but she felt strangely peaceful and eventually began to pray too. She asked God to welcome DB into heaven if it was his time, but mentioned that a miracle would be welcome. She prayed for her father, and then prayed for Bessy. *I know I'm asking a lot after a long absence, but please help me find Bessy and bring his murderers to justice.*

"Amen," Father Sebastian said and crossed himself.

"Amen," Grace said, squeezing her palms together to implore God for a few more moments before getting back up.

Returning to their cake, the priest asked after Suzanna and if she would be coming to his AA meetings. Grace had gone back to campus to check on her the day after the protests and found her hungover. Suzanna hadn't been at the riots after all, but talked excitedly about hosting a "Riotous Rioters" party. Grace tried not to feel let down. She recognized that it had been wishful thinking on her part because Suzanna *was* consistent. Her life was fun and games—a continuous party—and she was intent on stay-

ing in her silk cocoon. It was different for Grace; it had always been. Even in the best of times when her father was
still alive, working in the mines and sending money back
to the village every month, her good fortune felt precarious. It still did. She realized that Suzanna could never relate
because she had never experienced poverty. Once, when
Grace talked about how poor she had been in the village,
Suzanna spoke earnestly about how her father had once
cut her off for a whole month and she had been completely
broke too. Poverty and hardship were as abstract and re-
mote to Suzanna as luxury and insouciance were to Grace.
But if she hadn't known so much struggle and loss in her
life, would she still be able to feel other people's pain so
deeply? If Mr. Patel hadn't saved her life, would she care
so much about Bessy? If she hadn't had to fight so hard for
herself, would she feel compelled to fight for others? Or
was it in her DNA passed on from her father, as Mr. Patel
had claimed? Grace still loved Suzanna but something inside her had shifted. A close friendship with someone so
different in lifestyle, values and personal philosophy was
no longer tenable.

"I don't think Suzanna will be joining AA anytime
soon."

"Don't give up on her, Grace."

"No."

"Do you want the last piece of cake?"

"No thanks. I'm full."

Father Sebastian looked surprised. "Did you like the
stollen?"

"Is the Pope Catholic?"

Father Sebastian paused, thought about it, and then laughed and laughed.

23

"DB would want us to at least try to be dignified. Get off the floor now and blow your nose. You're getting mucus everywhere." Avaristo held out a handkerchief for Grace. His eyes were bloodshot from crying too, but he hadn't fallen to the floor and lain there wailing as Grace had.

She took the handkerchief and wiped her eyes and blew her nose. "I can't believe DB's gone," she kept repeating. DB's death was expected, but now that it had happened, it still hit her hard. Dread was poor preparation for grief. She folded the handkerchief and handed it back to Avaristo.

"Keep it. Please!" It was a soft deep blue silk, and almost as beautiful as the one she had given Bessy. "I have to go to the hospital and make sure that they don't move DB into that awful morgue. I can't bear the thought of him in there. The smell alone! They say there are so many bodies in there that they can get lost forever."

Something scratched at Grace's brain. Big Daddy had said the police were crafty but lazy. She knew that the family had checked the morgue once, but the police could have put Bessy in there anytime afterwards to get "lost" among the bodies.

"Can I come to the hospital with you?" Grace asked.

The horse-faced nurse told them that Mrs. Banda had already taken DB's body and transported it to a private morgue. "Our UTH morgue is the only one in Lusaka for poor people who are packed in there like kapenta. You rich ones have to have your own VIP morgues in Manda Hill and Kabulonga. Like it still matters when you're dead."

Avaristo looked like he was about to slap the nurse. "You're a disgrace to your profession and, believe you me, we're not done here."

The nurse said nothing, but her smug expression suggested that she had heard it all before, and she was still sitting in the VIP wing.

Avaristo raced off in his Peugeot. He didn't ask why Grace stayed behind and she didn't offer an explanation. Even before Grace got near the morgue, death felt close. She shivered. As she got closer, the stench forced her to stick her nose under her shirt. She knocked on the black metal double door with "Mortuary" written in white paint. A man in scrubs and a face mask opened it. Grace gagged and stepped back. He came out and closed the door behind him, and led her a distance away before pulling down his mask. It left its imprint on the skin beneath his red eyes and over the bridge of his nose.

"Can I help you?"

"I'm looking for someone in the morgue."

"This isn't a job for you. Bring a man, someone with a strong heart." He touched his chest.

"I have a strong heart." She raised her nose out of her shirt as if to prove it, but the smell was too bad and she fished Avaristo's handkerchief out of her bag to cover her nose again.

"Iai, sisi," he shook his head, "with the fridges not working properly, inde, it's not a job for anyone. There are so many bodies in there we have to pile them in the drawers." He sighed and wiped sweat off his bald head with his hand.

"Do the police bring bodies here?" Grace noticed that the man tensed up.

"Yes, victims of murder, hit-and-run, witchcraft. Shamu! So many smashed-up bodies."

"Do you remember the police bringing the body of a young man, very small in stature, like a boy, about this high." She raised her hand to the height of her armpit. "This would have been about eight months ago now."

"Eight months! Why did you take so long to come for him?"

"His father came, but his body wasn't here at the time. I want to check again. I need to."

"We don't keep bodies here for more than three months; then the City Council collects them."

"The City Council?"

"Yes, they collect unclaimed bodies and bury them in mass graves at the south end of Leopards Hill Cemetery. I'm sorry, sisi, but there are too many nowadays, too many to remember. If it was a police case, talk to N'gandu, he's the one dealing with the police. They only deal with him, and if he's not on duty, they'll come back. Like the rest of us aren't professionals." The man sucked his teeth.

Grace's heart began to race. Why would they only release bodies to one person unless… "I need to speak to N'gandu urgently. When's he next on duty?"

"He's inside there now." The man pointed back at the building with his chin. "I'll ask him to come out."

Grace escorted him to the door. "Wait here, sisi." He put his mask back on and ducked in. The stench through the open door was so overpowering Grace staggered away. She put her hands to her knees and waited for the urge to vomit to pass. She kept her eyes on the door until another man in scrubs emerged from the morgue. He approached her with his mouth and nose covered with a handkerchief folded into a triangle and tied across his head. On it, a leopard leapt across the universe of stars and planets.

Grace screamed, "My handkerchief!"

Leopards Hill Cemetery

October 1992

Epilogue

Grace stood beside a massive hole in the ground at the southern tip of the cemetery. The shovels had been cast aside now, and two men were on their hands and knees using trowels and their fingers to sift through the soil. They had exhumed over 100 bodies already, 102 to be precise, some full skeletons wrapped in tarpaulins, others bones and fragments scattered across meters of black earth. The men in the hole extracted skulls, ribs and finger and toe bones, and handed them to two other men in lab coats who brushed them, examined them and sorted them with clinical efficiency. The complete skeletons went into large opaque bags, and the other bones were organized into various coded boxes, macabre skeleton puzzles to be pieced back together later in a lab. A man in the hole lifted another skull out of the ground. It was number 103 and it had a bullet hole in its cranium.

It had taken a new President, a new regime, a new job as the youngest member of the Zambia Human Rights Commission and then more fighting to get here. To Grace's shock and dismay, the other commissioners had initially refused to exhume the bodies.

"President Chiluba wants us to focus on the future, not spend money digging up the ugly past," they had told Grace. She'd had to threaten to go to the new, independent newspaper with the Mulenga family before they capitulated. They were even more furious with her when they realized that now there wouldn't be enough money for them to attend a human rights workshop at the United Nations in New York. They began to spread rumors: that her boundless ambition made her ruthless; that she only got the job because she was President Chiluba's mistress; and, the only one that hurt her, that she had used Willbess's death to build her career and burnish her own star.

They had found Bessy's body early, near the surface, the smallest of all the skeletons. The seventh to be exhumed. As soon as the man opened the tarp, Grace knew it was him. She recognized his small frame curled up in the fetal position with black and red cloth still clinging to his skeleton, remnants of the same clothes he had worn when she met him. When the man lifted up his skull and Grace saw Bessy's chipped tooth, her knees buckled and she fell to the ground, where she stayed and wept for a long time.

She cried again at his funeral. Bessy should be alive and free in San Francisco. No! He should be alive and free in Lusaka, or Nyamphande, or wherever he chose to be. As

Father Sebastian recited the Prayer for the Dead, the Mulenga family clung to each other and seemed to hold each other upright. Grace felt hopeful for them, that they had each other and could survive their loss together. Mr. Patel put his arm around Grace, and Mrs. Njavwa took her hand and squeezed it tight. She had her family too.

Grace recognized only a few other people at the funeral. Godfredah stood not too far from her. His suit looked oversized, and his hair was now as short and as fine as a newborn baby. He looked so thin and frail that she could tell that Godfredah wouldn't be long for this world either. She thought she also saw Big Daddy out of the corner of her eye under a msolo tree, but when she looked again, he was gone. There were no politicians, no press and none of the other commissioners present when Bessy was reburied in a beautiful mukwa box on this side of Leopards Hill Cemetery, where dearly beloveds' names, years lived, and epitaphs were etched into tombstones.

Now Grace stood before a mass grave on the south side of the cemetery. A new President, a new regime and a Human Rights Commission didn't mean that the fight was won. Far from it. Officer "Munali" Muntu had been charged with Bessy's murder but was acquitted for lack of evidence. Her constitutional challenge to the Penal Code was languishing in the courts, with her hearing date delayed again and again. She received no support at all from the other commissioners, not since the canceled trip to the United Nations, and even President Chiluba declined her requests for a meeting and hadn't responded to her many letters asking for his help. Bessy had not been mentioned again publicly by the President or anyone else after the first days of his presidency over a year ago.

It had been two years since she met Bessy. She alone seemed to recognize the full importance of his life; beyond beloved son and brother, he was the catalyst that changed the history of Zambia. She knew that, but for him, President Kaunda would still be the President. He would never be known or revered like Gandhi or Mandela; he didn't fit the mold of a hero—his story too complicated, his death a bloody stain, far easier to cover than to own.

Grace knew that they were trying to erase Willbess "Bessy" Mulenga from Zambian history along with all the other people buried in these mass graves. She understood that the truth had to be told, the wrongs admitted, the injustices redressed before justice could be restored and the systems and the cycles of oppression ended once and for all. So she would continue to find skeletons, unearth their stories and, like the leopard, safeguard their spirits by making sure their existence lived on through remembrance and public exposure of what had happened to them. Grace understood that her job as a lawyer was to bear witness to these atrocities of the past, and to keep telling the truth, the whole truth, so help her God and her ancestors.

★ ★ ★ ★ ★

Acknowledgments

It takes a village to raise a novel and I am profoundly grateful to mine. My husband, David Lewis, who is my heart, my life partner and best friend; my other bestie, the brilliant writer Alexandra Fuller, who helped and encouraged me from beginning to end; my parents, Ilse and Jacob Mwanza, who raised me to love books, gave me the gift of education and served as my German and Nsenga translators; my sisters, Angela Mwanza and Namwali Serpell, who paved the way for this novel in so many ways; my advisors, Joyce Mwanza, Abigail Tembo, Patrick Bwalya and Gerry Lintini, the current, progressive Chief Nyamphande; Beth Bauman, who gave me my first lesson and my writing group; Brian Campbell, Nina Camp and Mitch Baranowski, who kept me going through the darkness of the pandemic; my agent, Ian Bonaparte, and the Janklow & Nesbit team for taking me on; my editors, Brittany Lavery and then Sara

Rogers at HarperCollins, and Ellah Wakatama at Canongate, whose wisdom and guidance got me and this book over the finish line.

Author's Note

The inspiration for this book is a decades-old haunting—a 1990s story in a Zambian newspaper in which the journalist described a boy beaten up by a mob in a central marketplace for wearing a dress. No one, at least according to the article, tried to protect or defend this adolescent from the attack; instead the tone was one of blame for "provoking" the crowd. I will never know what happened to him/her/them, but I do know from the many appalling reports that LGBTQ+ children, adolescents and adults across the world suffer from discrimination, hatred, violence and even death.

I wrote this book as a very belated response to the newspaper article that has stayed with me for decades. While I knew that I was ill-equipped to tell such a story from the point of view of an LGBTQ+ character—and fortunately there are others telling these important stories—I felt well qualified to tell the story of Grace, a young lawyer defending her client Willbess "Bessy" Mulenga for crimes "against the order of nature." While this book is fiction, the penal code criminalizing gay sex is real, and is still the law in Zambia and many jurisdictions around the world.

Like with that young person in the newspaper, in this book we never find out Bessy's full history; this story is told from Grace's perspective, so we only know what she knows, see what she sees and understand the world as it was in Zambia in the 1980s/90s, before there was the language of queerness. She has a hard-earned law degree yet, as a victim of poverty, class and gender discrimination, is herself vulnerable. Despite this vulnerability, or perhaps because of it, she understands a universal truth: that the fight for the rights and humanity of Bessy *is a fight for the rights and humanity of us all.*

Through stories, we can cast light on what baffles, haunts, hurts and can destroy us, and good stories enable us to learn, debate, heal and move in the direction of understanding and grace. That's my hope for *The Lions' Den.*